STAR FLEET DATABANK HARDCOPY

STAR TREK
MR. SCOTT'S
GUIDE TO THE
ENTERPRISE ™

STAR TREK

MR. SCOTT'S GUIDE TO THE ENTERPRISE ™

Written and illustrated by Shane Johnson
Based upon the engineering logs of Chief Engineer Montgomery Scott

POCKET BOOKS

New York   London   Toronto   Sydney   Tokyo

An *Original* Publication of POCKET BOOKS

POCKET BOOKS, a division of Simon & Schuster Inc., 1230 Avenue of the Americas, New York, NY 10020

ISBN: 0-671-63576-X

First Pocket Books trade paperback printing July 1987

10 9 8 7 6 5

ACKNOWLEDGMENTS

This author wishes to thank the following people for the assistance and encouragement which made this book possible:

Michael Okuda, designer of the display graphics on the Star Trek IV Enterprise bridge, who served as technical consultant for this project

Andrew Probert, designer for Star Trek: The Motion Picture, who provided not only production sketches but also rare insights into those sections of Enterprise never seen on-screen

David Kimble, whose cutaway illustration of Enterprise proved to be an invaluable reference

Ralph Winter, executive producer for Star Trek IV, whose kindness and patience made possible my research at Paramount's Star Trek soundstages

Dave Stern, editor at Pocket Books, who put in almost as many hours on this project as I did and went beyond the call of duty in its production

Amy Rayfiel, of Paramount's merchandising department, who made sure that I was provided with studio stills and more set drawings than I could carry

Paul Newitt, whose assistance in the early stages of this project helped get the ball rolling

Reg Martin, whose unequalled support over the past two years made this book possible from the beginning

Kathy Johnson, my wife, who repeatedly managed to keep our two-year-old, Daniel, from coloring on his father's technical illustrations

Also contributing were:

Lawrence Aeschlimann, Richard Arnold, Alan Beckner, Bob and Kathy Burns, James Chambers, Mark and Patti Elrod, Allen Everhart, David Holt, Shaun Johnson, Bob and Linda Klem, Walter Koenig, Mike Kott, Ret and Earlene Martin, Steve McClellan, Larry Oler, Don Punchatz, Barry Smith, and Rick Sternbach.

Special thanks to the members of Metrostar 1975:

Mark Brey, Mark Cheney, Harry Cooper, Richard Daniel, Mike Eckey, Kathy Hansen, Jerri Hopkins, Doug Klein, Melinda Lusk, Jan Malone, Carrie Mayfield, Cindy McConnell, Paul Opitz, Tony Rodriguez, Kenny Simmons, Richard Standlee, Lee Vinson, and Chris Van Vlake

Preliminary design sketches by Andrew Probert
Illustrations on pages 15-19, 96, 97, 100, 101 by David Kimble
Workbee logo by Chris Elliot
Star Trek IV bridge display graphics on pages 118-124 by Michael Okuda
Logos and symbols on pages 35-39 by Lee Cole
Special materials provided by Forest Brown, FASA Corporation

For Dan
Little did we know twelve years ago
...Maranatha, old friend

CONTENTS

INTRODUCTION

On behalf of the officers and crew of the starship Enterprise, I would like to take this opportunity to welcome you to your first tour of duty aboard this vessel. You may take pride in the fact that you are among the distinguished few among Star Fleet's ranks to be given such an assignment— service aboard a starship, the mission successes of which have become almost legendary.

This manual has been provided that you might more easily acquaint yourself with life aboard Enterprise, the flagship of the Enterprise class and one of the most sophisticated vessels in the fleet. You may have served aboard a ship of the Constitution class (the class to which Enterprise previously belonged) during your career; perhaps you are newly graduated from Star Fleet Academy. In any case, this manual will prove to be an invaluable guide to officers and crew alike.

Deck by deck, in full detail, this book will familiarize you with the interior arrangement of this vessel, thus allowing you to "ease into" your new position with greater comfort and efficiency. The interior and exterior differences between the old Enterprise and the new, as you have probably noticed, are striking indeed; in fact, only a few of the core structural support systems in the primary hull have actually survived the refit and are integrated into the new design. She's almost an entirely new lass, and as such Enterprise is well on her way to breaking every speed and success record she ever set.

She's a tall ship, and I'm proud to have served as primary designer during her rebirth. Improved warp, phaser, and deflector performance have been incorporated into the new configuration (as will be explained in the text of this book), making Enterprise the most powerful single active vessel known to the Federation. This distinction is indeed a reflection upon you, for the pride of the fleet is manned only by the pride of the fleet.

Again, welcome aboard. With your help, Enterprise will boldly pursue her ongoing mission, and will, as stated in the Star Fleet charter, venture "where no man has gone before."

Commander Montgomery Scott
Chief Engineer
U.S.S. Enterprise

HISTORY OF REFIT

On April 7, 2212 [Enterprise stardate 7523.2], the Constitution class U.S.S. Enterprise returned to Earth orbit following her last historic five-year mission. In doing so, the vessel earned a distinction unparalleled in Star Fleet history; of the original thirteen Constitution class vessels launched, Enterprise alone had not been lost or destroyed in the line of duty. This fact graphically displayed to the general public that starship exploration was indeed far more dangerous than generally thought, and as a result the ship and her crew rose to the status of living legend.

In the public eye, Enterprise became the recognized symbol for Star Fleet and the Federation in general. This consensus, followed by a motion by the Federation Council, led Star Fleet to reverse a decision made, unknown to the public, three months earlier; Enterprise was to have been decommissioned and disassembled following her return.

Though Enterprise had been reprieved, she was still twenty-five years old and her on-board technology was outdated. The vessel had undergone four overhauls since her initial launch in 2190, but these scheduled drydock periods had simply repaired her existing systems without introducing newer technologies (as was Star Fleet standard procedure at the time). It quickly became obvious that only a major refit could keep Enterprise at the forefront of the fleet.

Even as Enterprise approached drydock, Leeding Engines Ltd. successfully completed its final tests on a new warp nacelle configuration, the first real breakthrough in warp technology in fourteen years. Chief Engineer Montgomery Scott proposed that Enterprise be the first Federation vessel to be fitted with the new engines and, following an endorsement by Star Fleet Engineering Command, preparations were made for delivery of the new FWG-1 nacelles.

Leeding's FWG-1 engines differed greatly from the Shuvinaaljis Warp Technologies Model FWF-1 nacelles which had so faithfully served Enterprise during her twenty-five years. The FWF-1 units had not only been designed to generate the warp envelope through which the vessel would travel, but also contained individual thrust systems which propelled the ship forward. These propulsion units, which operated independently from the impulse deck on the primary hull, allowed the secondary hull to serve as a self-propelled lifeboat in the event of catastrophic primary hull damage. This option, never used by any Federation starship, came at the sacrifice of a great amount of generated energy which, channeled into the nacelle propulsion units, could otherwise have been used for increased phaser, deflector, and warp field capabilities.

Leeding's new FWG-1 warp drive system took a different, somewhat more efficient approach. The nacelles, fed by a linear intermix system contained within the body of the secondary hull, functioned solely as warp field generator units. All propulsive

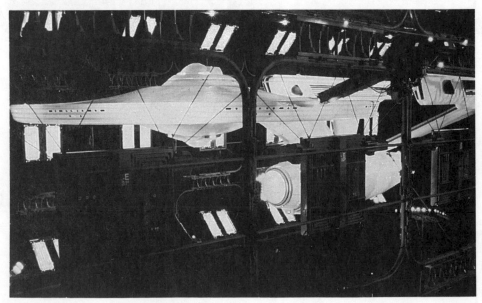

**Enterprise within Drydock Facility Three
(July 2216)**

energies were fed through the impulse drive system, the sole source of drive thrust. This arrangement not only reduced structural stress in the nacelle pylons and secondary hull strongback, but also provided thirty-three percent more operating power and greatly increased the vessel's range.

Computer simulations showed that Enterprise's existing nacelle support pylons were of insufficient diameter to contain the new warp drive shaft; nor would they structurally bear the mass of the FWG-1 nacelles. Further testing revealed that a new secondary hull/nacelle support pylon configuration was required before the heavier engines and their new intermix shaft could be incorporated into Enterprise.

What began as an engineering refit evolved into a redesign of the entire vessel. This created many major changes in the ship's appearance and led to the development of several new shipboard systems, created exclusively for Enterprise. Since the secondary hull would no longer serve as a lifeboat, it no longer needed to contain duplicates of the deck-by-deck features of the primary hull; all crew's quarters were eliminated, as were recreational facilities and most science labs. Eliminating this redundancy factor allowed for the creation of an expanded cargo deck which could accomodate Star Fleet's new standardized cargo module system; access to the new cargo deck was improved by enlarging the hangar deck and incorporating a one-way force field barrier which contained the ship's atmosphere while the hangar doors were open.

The external navigational deflector dish was eliminated and replaced with a more powerful, enclosed unit. Also, Star Fleet's standardized docking port system was added at the A, H, M, and Q Deck levels, and a particle-thrust reaction-control system was installed at strategic points on Enterprise's hull.

The starship's primary hull presented a particular challenge to Commander Scott and the designing engineers. Enterprise's existing M-4 computer was inadequate to the task of handling the ship's new propulsion and deflector systems, and as Leeding Engines Ltd. had designed the FWG-1 around Daystrom Data Concepts' M-6 logic system, the new computer would have to be installed aboard Enterprise. Unlike the M-4 (which occupied the central areas of levels 7 and 8), the M-6 computer was housed in a central core shaft eight feet in diameter. This shaft extended all the way through the primary hull, physically connecting the base of the helm con-

sole on the main bridge with an improved sensor array complex at the bottom of the saucer.

The new impulse deck, built by Kloratis Drives of Alpha Centauri (in conjunction with Leeding Engines Ltd.), incorporated an impulse deflection crystal which channeled thrust energy from the vertical intermix chamber directly into a Model FIE-2 tandem impulse unit. Five independently-ejectable fusion reactors, housed between the impulse engines, provided power and impulse thrust energy in the event of an emergency hull separation.

Several locations were proposed for an enlarged recreation deck. E Deck was at one time considered, as was T Deck (in a location which eventually became a botanical garden). Eventually the facility was placed in the rim of the saucer, just starboard of the impulse deck.

During the refit, Enterprise was given an additional, though minor, footnote in Star Fleet history. In order to save adding many tons of mass to the vessel, it was decided, for the first time ever, not to paint a Federation vessel with the customary light-gray thermocoat. In fact, Enterprise's pearlescent, bare-alloy appearance was so favorably received that Star Fleet has eliminated thermocoat from all vessels of 90,000 metric tons and above.

Shipboard weapons systems were also updated. Phaser power was dramatically increased by chan-

Forward secondary hull and photorp launch system

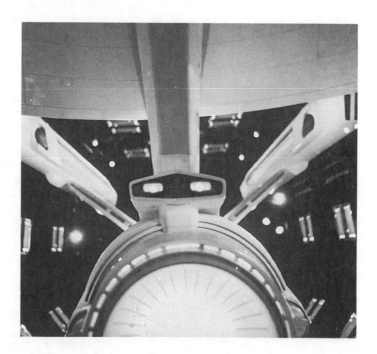

neling energy directly from the warp nacelles at a point beyond the dilithium/magnatomic-initiator stage. Phaser fire can be adjusted to deliver tight-or wide-beam, steady-stream or pulse energy; beam force is adjustable, ranging from disintegrate to light stun. Antimatter imbalance within the warp nacelles would result in a cutoff of phaser power under the new design; as a backup, the photon torpedo system, installed at the base of the connecting dorsal, was designed to draw from a separate system for use in case of a major phaser loss.

An untested defense system, verified by computer, was chosen to protect Enterprise from whatever hostile action she might encounter. Her main deflector shields, made possible by a breakthrough in Federation defense technology, were designed to be stronger and more resilient than any in use. In this new technology, a coil of diburnium-osmium alloy [a substance created by the lost Kalandan race; discovered on Stardate 5978.2 by the Enterprise crew and recorded by Science Officer Spock] was placed within a reinforced titanium/transparent aluminum mount, scanned at the subatomic level, then replicated and projected as energy at an adjustable point beyond the vessel's outer hull. This energy layer, acting as a solid, in effect became another layer of metal on the ship's exterior. Insulated from the true hull by a small space, the invisible shield was designed to replenish its "molecular" structure continually for as long as source energy was available.

A secondary defense field, coil-generated, was designed for Enterprise which would form a "bubble" to provide secondary reinforcement in the protection of A, B, and C Decks.

As a final line of defense, to prevent capture, Enterprise was designed to incorporate two separate self-destruct systems. The proposed first of these, to be used only in deep space and clear of all planetary bodies, involved the total shutdown of all magnetic insulation systems in the linear intermix chamber and in all antimatter storage bottles. The planned result was an uncontrolled detonation and chain reaction, engulfing any ship or other body near the sun-like fireball. The ship's computer would be programmed to execute this procedure if the last two words in the destruct command were "destruct one."

The secondary self-destruct plan, to be used in planetary orbit or when too near any other object to be preserved, resulted in the detonation of specially placed charges throughout the ship. All antimatter bottles were to be ejected intact, and then escape along a course chosen during the last minute by the ship's computer. All breakers would be overridden, and all onboard electrical and computer systems would overload and detonate. Finally, powerful charges within the hull were to destroy the superstructure and render the ship a lifeless hulk, useless to enemy captors. The ship's computer would be programmed to execute this procedure if the last two words in the destruct command were "destruct zero."

Both of these destruct plans were approved and incorporated into Enterprise.

SPECIFICATIONS

OVERALL LENGTH	990.6 FT	SHIP'S COMPLIMENT	
OVERALL DRAFT	231.7 FT	OFFICERS	72
OVERALL BEAM	460.5 FT	ENLISTED [CREW]	428
PRIMARY HULL [SAUCER]		PERFORMANCE	
LENGTH	475.4 FT	MAXIMUM VELOCITY	WARP 12 [1728c]
DRAFT	106.9 FT	CRUISING VELOCITY	WARP 8 [512c]
BEAM [DIAMETER]	460.5 FT		
		ACCELERATION	
SECONDARY HULL [ENGINEERING]		0-.99c	19 SECONDS
LENGTH	393.2 FT	.99c- WARP	1.1 SECONDS
DRAFT	154.3 FT	ENGAGE	
BEAM	106.9 FT	WARP 1-4	.78 SECONDS
		WARP 4-8	.67 SECONDS
NACELLES [LEEDING FWG-1]		WARP 8-12	2.13 SECONDS
LENGTH	503.1 FT		
DRAFT	54.9 FT		
BEAM	40.9 FT		

REACTION-CONTROL THRUSTERS

SPACE-ENERGY/MATTER SINK (ACQUISITION)

MAGNATOMIC FLUX CONSTRUCTION—FIRST STAGE

POWER-STAGE MAGNATOMIC FLUX CHILLER (OUTBOARD)

EMERGENCY FLUSH VENTS

EMERGENCY FLUSH INTAKES

LANDING-BAY CONTROL ROOM

LANDING-BAY DOORS

LATERAL DEFLECTOR GRID (ENGINEERING)

WARP ENGINE NACELLE

DOCKING PORT EXHAUST

DOCKING PORT —ENGINEERING

IMPULSE ENGINE

PRIMARY DOCKING PORT

V.I.P. LOUNGE WINDOWS

CONNECTING DORSAL

PHOTON TORPEDO TUBES

REACTION-CONTROL THRUSTERS

SPACE-ENERGY FIELD ATTRACTION SENSORS

FORWARD PHASER BANKS

MAIN GANGWAY HATCH

PRIMARY FORCE-FIELD DEFLECTOR

PROFILE

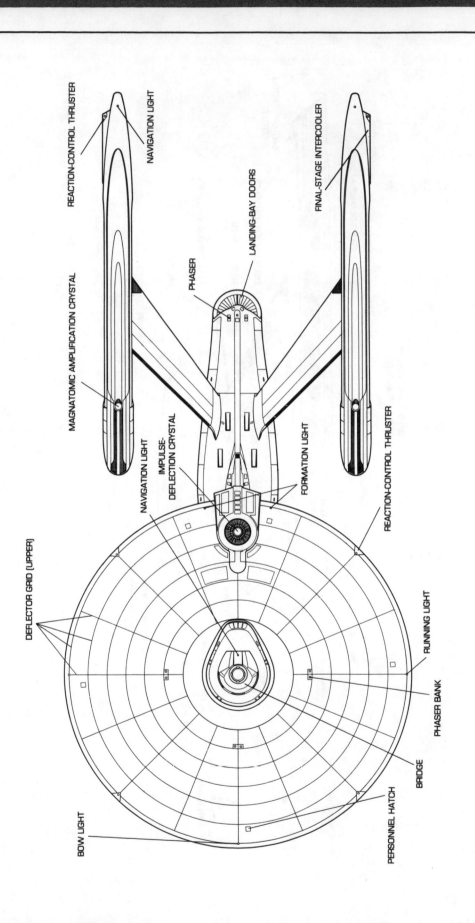

TOP VIEW

REACTION-CONTROL THRUSTER

NAVIGATION LIGHT

MAGNATOMIC AMPLIFICATION CRYSTAL

PHASER

LANDING-BAY DOORS

FINAL-STAGE INTERCOOLER

NAVIGATION LIGHT

IMPULSE-DEFLECTION CRYSTAL

FORMATION LIGHT

REACTION-CONTROL THRUSTER

DEFLECTOR GRID (UPPER)

RUNNING LIGHT

PHASER BANK

BRIDGE

PERSONNEL HATCH

BOW LIGHT

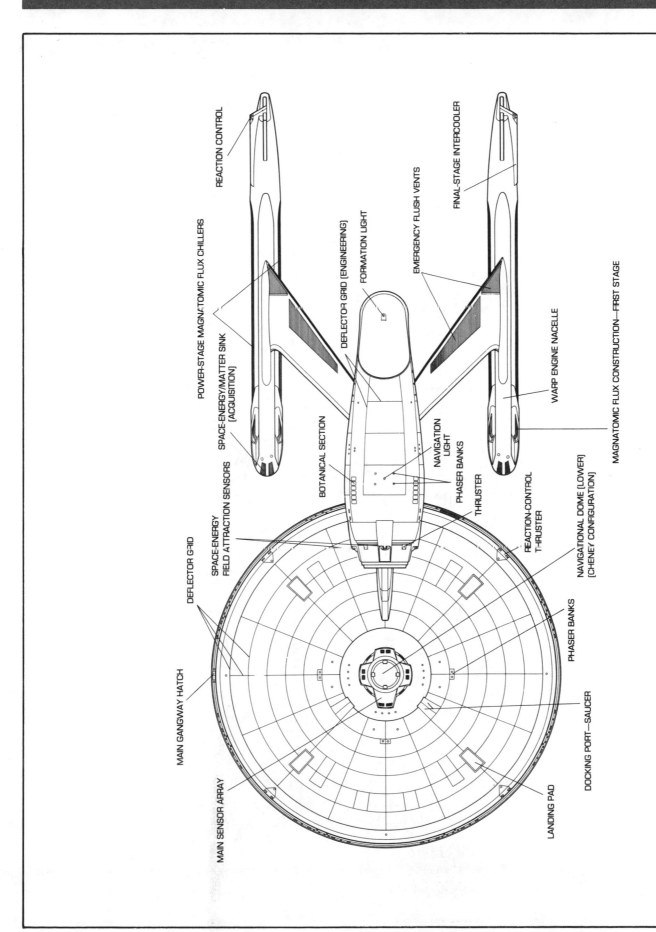

BOTTOM VIEW

REACTION CONTROL

POWER-STAGE MAGNATOMIC FLUX CHILLERS

SPACE-ENERGY/MATTER SINK [ACQUISITION]

DEFLECTOR GRID [ENGINEERING]

FORMATION LIGHT

EMERGENCY FLUSH VENTS

FINAL-STAGE INTERCOOLER

WARP ENGINE NACELLE

MAGNATOMIC FLUX CONSTRUCTION—FIRST STAGE

BOTANICAL SECTION

NAVIGATION LIGHT

PHASER BANKS

THRUSTER

REACTION-CONTROL T-THRUSTER

NAVIGATIONAL DOME [LOWER] [CHENEY CONFIGURATION]

DEFLECTOR GRID

SPACE-ENERGY FIELD ATTRACTION SENSORS

MAIN GANGWAY HATCH

MAIN SENSOR ARRAY

PHASER BANKS

DOCKING PORT—SAUCER

LANDING PAD

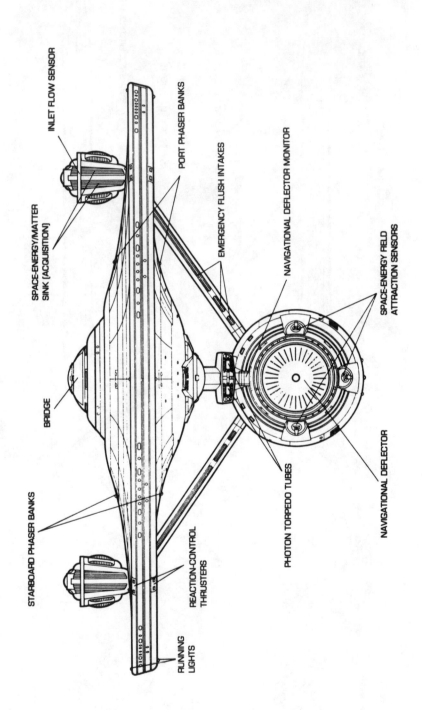

INLET FLOW SENSOR

SPACE-ENERGY/MATTER SINK (ACQUISITION)

PORT PHASER BANKS

EMERGENCY FLUSH INTAKES

NAVIGATIONAL DEFLECTOR MONITOR

SPACE-ENERGY FIELD ATTRACTION SENSORS

BRIDGE

STARBOARD PHASER BANKS

REACTION-CONTROL THRUSTERS

RUNNING LIGHTS

PHOTON TORPEDO TUBES

NAVIGATIONAL DEFLECTOR

BOW

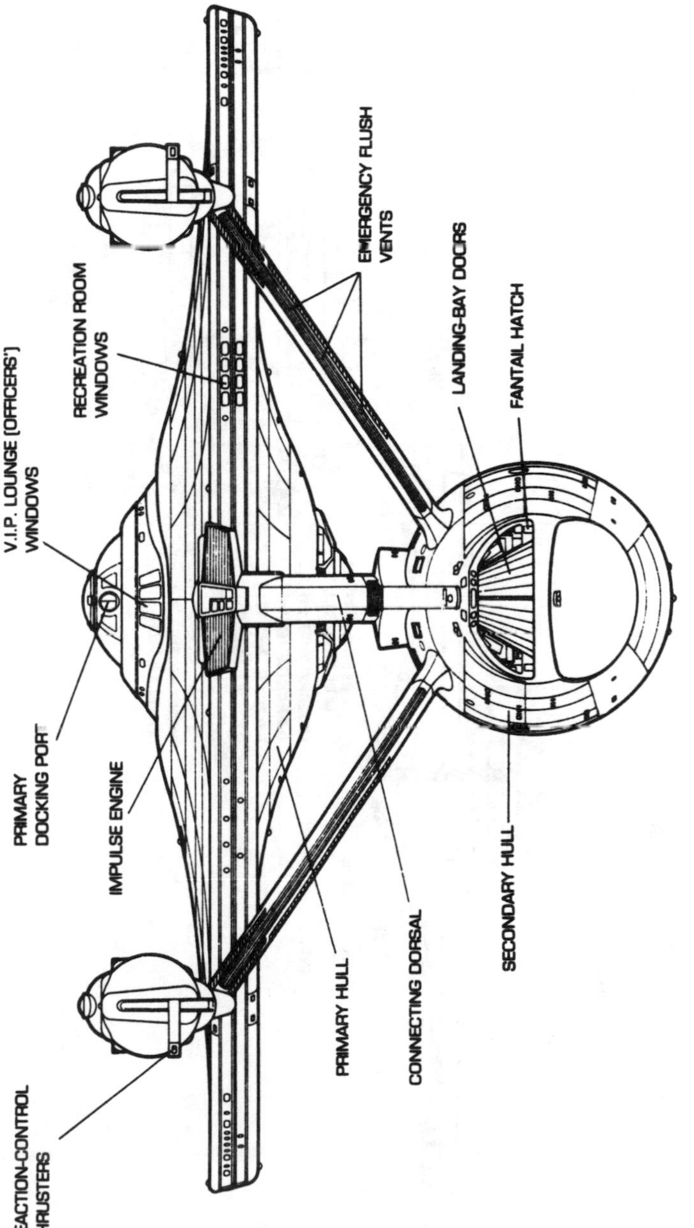

REACTION-CONTROL THRUSTERS

PRIMARY DOCKING PORT

V.I.P. LOUNGE (OFFICERS') WINDOWS

RECREATION ROOM WINDOWS

EMERGENCY FLUSH VENTS

IMPULSE ENGINE

PRIMARY HULL

CONNECTING DORSAL

LANDING-BAY DOORS

FANTAIL HATCH

SECONDARY HULL

STERN

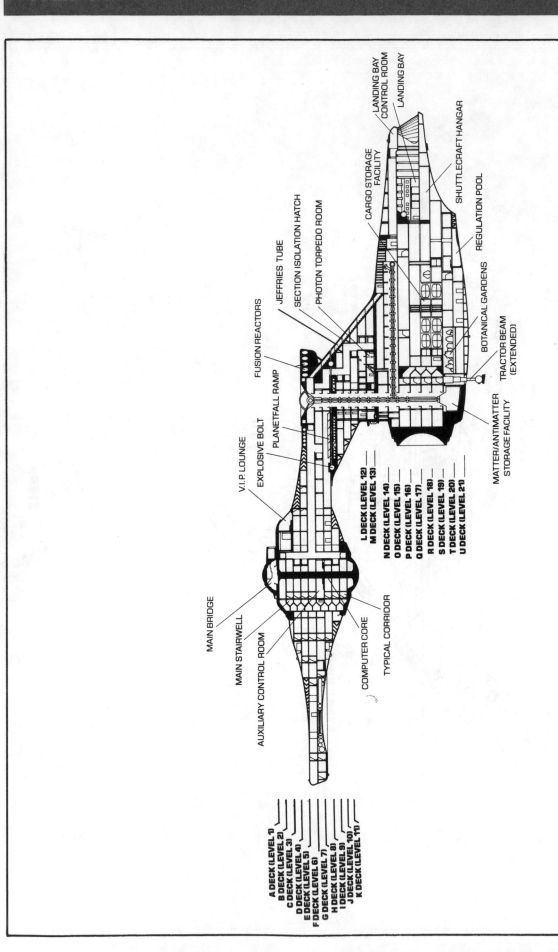

LANDING BAY CONTROL ROOM
LANDING BAY
CARGO STORAGE FACILITY
SHUTTLECRAFT HANGAR
REGULATION POOL
JEFFRIES TUBE
SECTION ISOLATION HATCH
PHOTON TORPEDO ROOM
BOTANICAL GARDENS
TRACTOR BEAM (EXTENDED)
FUSION REACTORS
MATTER/ANTIMATTER STORAGE FACILITY
PLANETFALL RAMP
V.I.P. LOUNGE
EXPLOSIVE BOLT
MAIN BRIDGE
MAIN STAIRWELL
AUXILIARY CONTROL ROOM
COMPUTER CORE
TYPICAL CORRIDOR

A DECK (LEVEL 1)
B DECK (LEVEL 2)
C DECK (LEVEL 3)
D DECK (LEVEL 4)
E DECK (LEVEL 5)
F DECK (LEVEL 6)
G DECK (LEVEL 7)
H DECK (LEVEL 8)
I DECK (LEVEL 9)
J DECK (LEVEL 10)
K DECK (LEVEL 11)

L DECK (LEVEL 12)
M DECK (LEVEL 13)
N DECK (LEVEL 14)
O DECK (LEVEL 15)
P DECK (LEVEL 16)
Q DECK (LEVEL 17)
R DECK (LEVEL 18)
S DECK (LEVEL 19)
T DECK (LEVEL 20)
U DECK (LEVEL 21)

INBOARD PROFILE

CONTRACTORS' SKETCHES

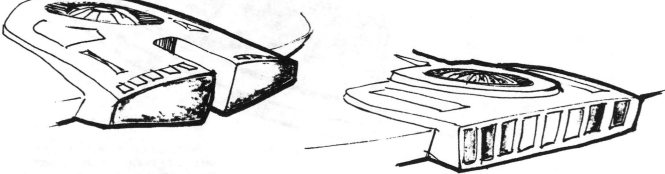

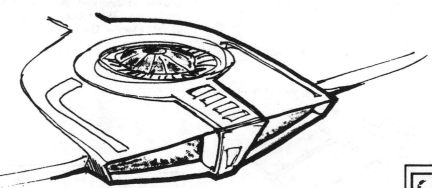

Proposed housings for the new FIE-2 tandem impulse deck included the arrangements shown above. [Sketches courtesy of Kloratis Drives Corp.]

	UNITED FEDERATION OF PLANETS **STAR FLEET DIVISION** SYSTEM - SOL / EARTH SAN FRANCISCO, NO. AM.	
CONTRACTOR'S PROPOSED DESIGN		
VESSEL: U.S.S. ENTERPRISE		CLASS: ENTERPRISE
RELEASED: 17 DEC 2214	PROJECT: IMPULSE DECK CONFIGURATION	
EXECUTED: PROJECT ENGINEER *Peter Burke*	AUTHENTICATED: PRIMARY DESIGNER *Adam Rozer*	
CONTRACTOR: KLORATIS DRIVES CORP.		
VIEW: EXTERIOR		SHT 1 OF 1

CONTRACTORS' SKETCHES

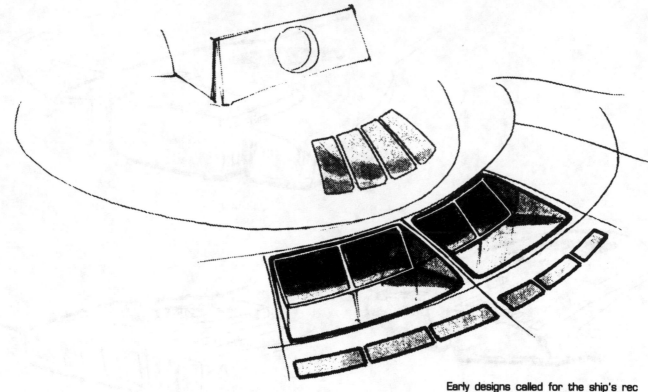

Early designs called for the ship's rec deck to be located aft on D-E Decks. These viewport configurations would provide an overhead view for off-duty personnel. [Sketches courtesy of Chiokis Starship Construction Corp.]

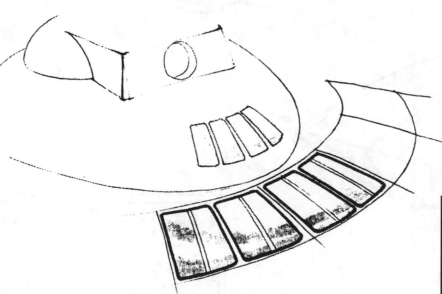

UNITED FEDERATION OF PLANETS
STAR FLEET DIVISION
SYSTEM - SOL / EARTH
SAN FRANCISCO, NO. AM.

CONTRACTOR'S PROPOSED DESIGN

VESSEL: U.S.S. ENTERPRISE	CLASS: ENTERPRISE
RELEASED: 3 JUN 2212	PROJECT: REC DECK WINDOWS
EXECUTED: PROJECT ENGINEER	AUTHENTICATED: PRIMARY DESIGNER

CONTRACTOR:

CHIOKIS STARSHIP CONSTRUCTION CORP.

| VIEW: EXTERIOR | SHT 1 OF 1 |

GENERAL INFORMATION

DUTY UNIFORMS

The great success of Enterprise's historic five-year mission brought other changes to Star Fleet procedure. To honor the ship and her crew, Star Fleet Command unanimously elected in 2212 to drop the individual ship emblem system employed since 2206 and then adopt the insignia of Enterprise (Command Division) as the official insignia of Star Fleet. Each individual's branch department would no longer be denoted by shirt color; rather, this would be expressed by a colored, circular background on the uniform insignia. The basic uniform became a long-sleeved tunic of gray or tan, with foot coverings built into the uniform pants.

This uniform, used until 2219, proved unpopular with officers and enlisted personnel alike, as well as with the press and public. In an attempt to get back to the much-liked tunic/pants/boots combination, Star Fleet designers proposed a new concept; a wraparound tunic, maroon in color, would cover a long-sleeved undershirt, the color of which would denote branch department. The long-standing system of denoting rank by sleeve stripes was dropped in favor of a rank pin to be worn on the shoulder and left sleeve of the proposed tunic. Black pants and boots, similar to those used prior to 2212, and an insignia pin to be worn on the left breast of the tunic were added, as was a black belt with buckle.

The new uniform styling was adopted in September of 2219. Several matching items of off-duty and landing party clothing were issued as well, giving Star Fleet officers an impressive, unified appearance. Several members of the press argued that the new uniforms were too militaristic in design, thus conflicting with the Federation's stand that Star Fleet was primarily an organization of exploration and discovery. This stirred protest among several Terran peace-seeking groups who felt that Star Fleet was already taking too little action to resolve the long-standing conflict with the Klingon Empire, but these concerns were unfounded and subsided quickly.

Also added to the new uniform, on the forearm of the left sleeve, was a service bar which denoted the wearer's length of service. A cluster of one- and five-year pins, arranged at the wearer's discretion, were issued, with others to be issued annually.

UNIFORM COLOR CODES

01 SILVER	21 VIOLET
02 ANTIMONY	22 CORN
03 GOLD	23 TAN
04 BRONZE	24 BROWN
05 COPPER	25 NUDE
06 WHITE	26 PURPLE
07 IVORY	27 OXIDE
08 SAND	28 TAUPE
09 BLOOD	29 PLATINUM
10 RED	30 GRAY
11 ORANGE	31 BLUEGRAY
12 YELLOW	32 BLACK
13 TENNE	33 SILVER BLUE
14 OLIVE	34 GRAY-GREEN
15 GREEN	35 SALMON
16 SKY BLUE	36 BUFF
17 ULTRAMARINE	37 PEARL
18 BLUE	38 MAHOGANY
19 INDIGO	39 NAVY
20 MIDNIGHT	40 BURGUNDY

KEY TO SYMBOLS

(01) NUMBER IN CIRCLE REPRESENTS ITEM COLOR

(D) INDICATES ITEM IS DEPARTMENT COLOR

DEPARTMENT COLORS

06 COMMAND
16 SCIENCES
03 SERVICES [ENGINEERING, SECURITY, OTHER]
14 MEDICAL
30 OPERATIONS
10 CADET

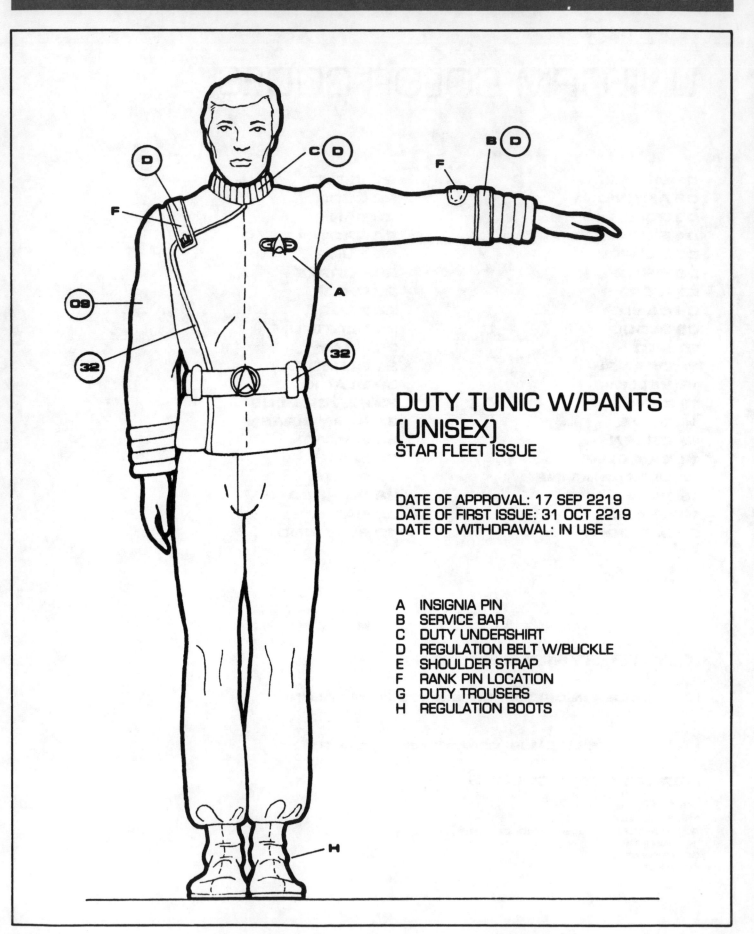

DUTY TUNIC W/PANTS [UNISEX]
STAR FLEET ISSUE

DATE OF APPROVAL: 17 SEP 2219
DATE OF FIRST ISSUE: 31 OCT 2219
DATE OF WITHDRAWAL: IN USE

A   INSIGNIA PIN
B   SERVICE BAR
C   DUTY UNDERSHIRT
D   REGULATION BELT W/BUCKLE
E   SHOULDER STRAP
F   RANK PIN LOCATION
G   DUTY TROUSERS
H   REGULATION BOOTS

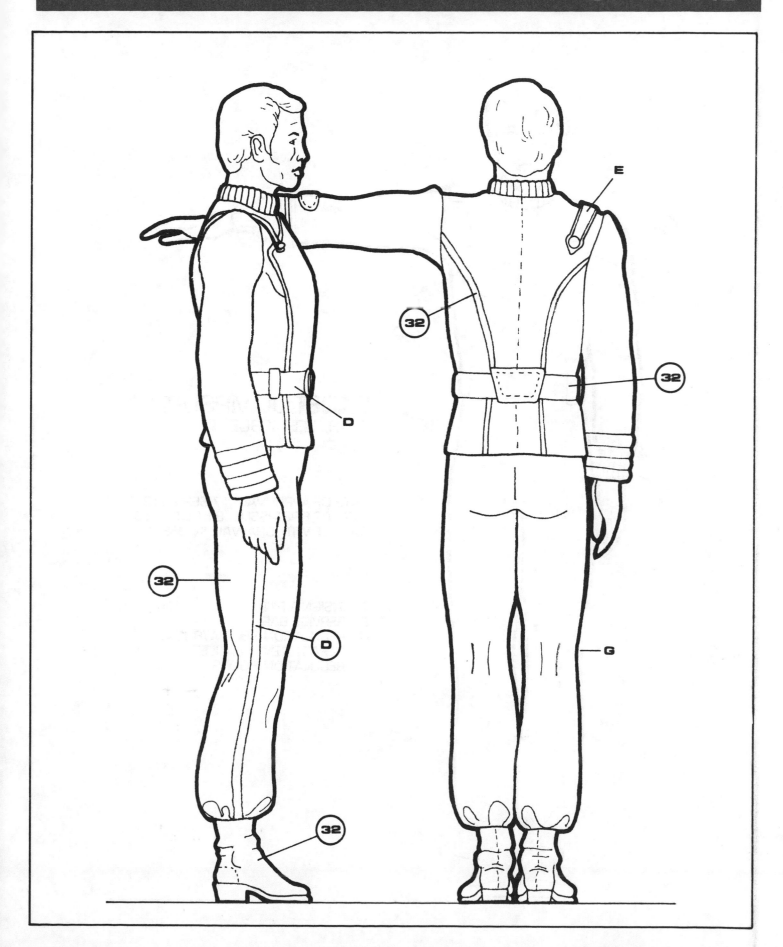

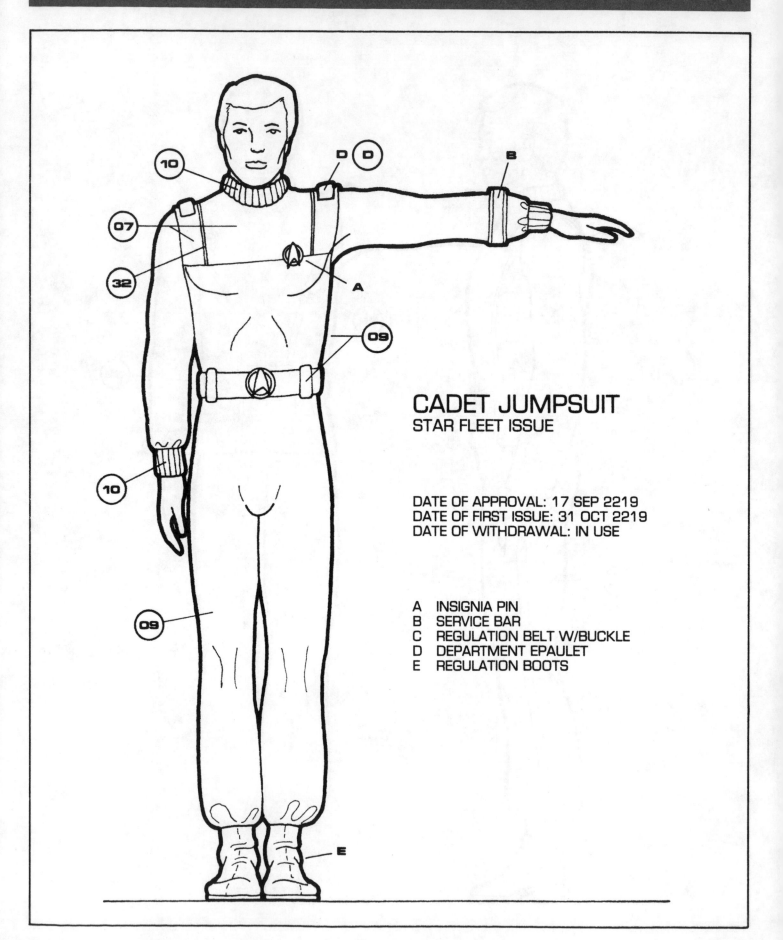

CADET JUMPSUIT
STAR FLEET ISSUE

DATE OF APPROVAL: 17 SEP 2219
DATE OF FIRST ISSUE: 31 OCT 2219
DATE OF WITHDRAWAL: IN USE

A   INSIGNIA PIN
B   SERVICE BAR
C   REGULATION BELT W/BUCKLE
D   DEPARTMENT EPAULET
E   REGULATION BOOTS

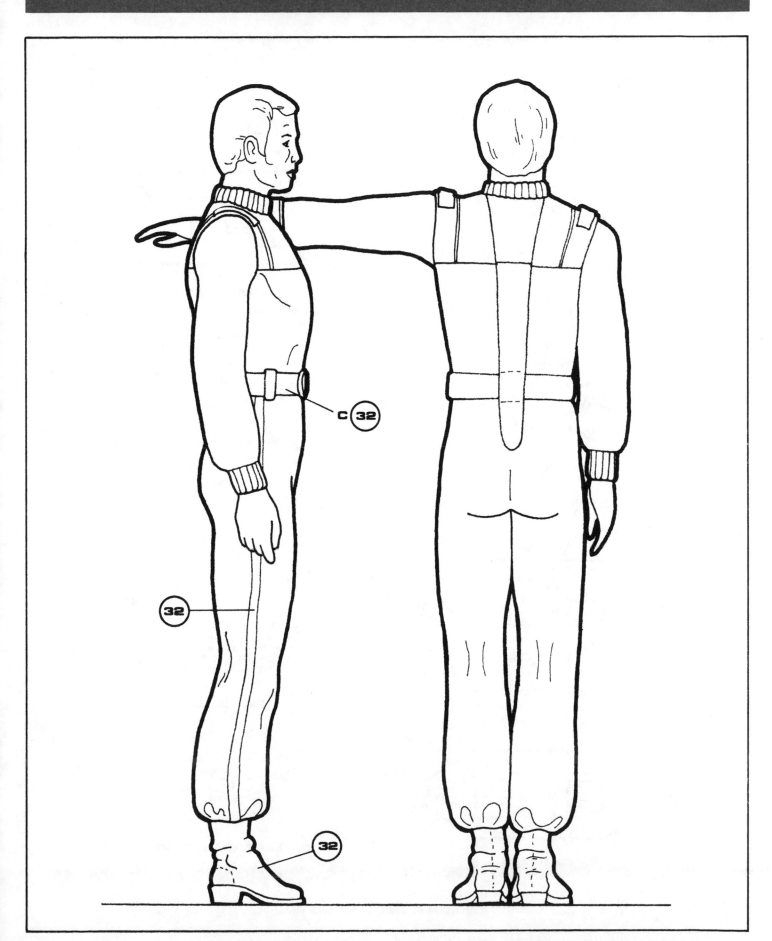

RANK PINS

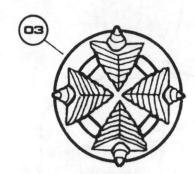

FLEET ADMIRAL

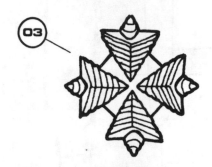

ADMIRAL

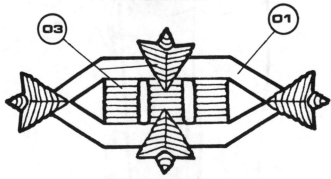

COMMODORE

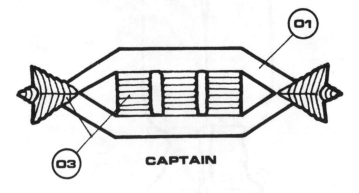

CAPTAIN

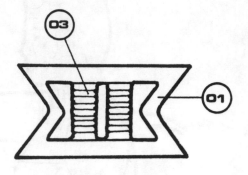

COMMANDER

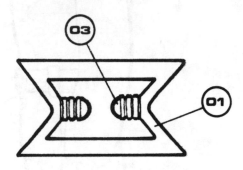

LT. COMMANDER

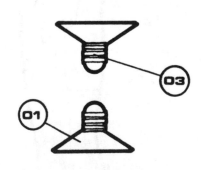

LIEUTENANT

LIEUTENANT JG

ENSIGN RANK HAS NO PIN

SERVICE BARS

SERVICE BAR WITH PINS DISPLAYED
(PINS DENOTE NINETEEN YEARS OF SERVICE)

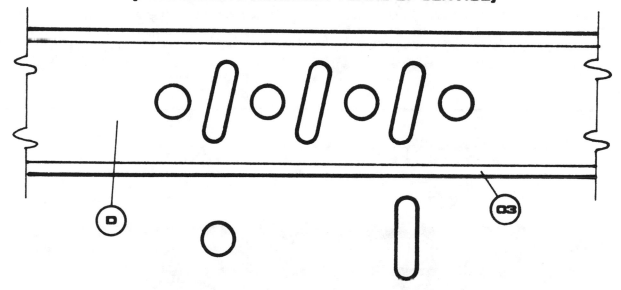

ONE-YEAR PIN   **FIVE-YEAR PIN**

FIRST YEAR SERVICE BAR
(ANGLED STRIPE IS OFFICER'S DEPARTMENT COLOR)

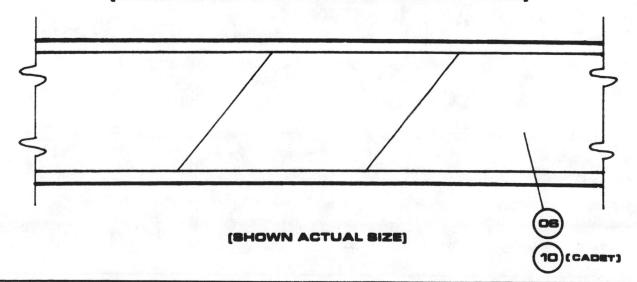

(SHOWN ACTUAL SIZE)

TYPEFACES

Prior to November of 2210, all Federation hull markings were rendered in a typestyle known as Machine Extended. These markings, letters and numerals alike, were painted in black over the vessel's light gray thermocoat and often were accompanied by the red and yellow Star Fleet banner.

In 2210, it was decided that a change would be made in order to accompany the new vessel designs being produced. To this end, a new typeface was created and designated as Star Fleet Bold Extended. Its characters, generally rendered in black with a red outline, lent a new image to Star Fleet hulls and complimented the lines of the new generation of vessels.

Also accepted for hull and interior bulkhead use were the typestyles of Microgramma and Microgramma Bold Extended. These styles, along with Helvetica Medium and Microgramma Medium Extended, comprise all screen display and hardcopy printout texts aboard ship.

STAR FLEET BOLD EXTENDED

A B C D E F G
H I J K L M N
O P Q R S T U
V W X Y Z
1 2 3 4 5 6 7 8
9 0 & ? [ ] ! : ; " , _

MICROGRAMMA

A B C D E F G H I
J K L M N O P Q
R S T U V W X Y Z
1 2 3 4 5 6 7
8 9 0 & ? ( ) ! : ; ".-

MICROGRAMMA BOLD EXTENDED

A B C D E F G H I
J K L M N O P Q R
S T U V W X Y Z
1 2 3 4 5 6 7
8 9 0 & ? ( ) ! : ; ".-

GRAPHICS LABELS

In order to assist new crew members as they familiarize themselves with the internal arrangement of Enterprise, a new system of graphic labelling has been adopted aboard ship. Foremost among the new symbols used is a set of department logos. These emblems, denoting the various operations departments aboard Federation vessels, appear in all related sections of the ship, as well as on equipment and subsystems located within those sections. For example, the Science Department logo appears on the doors leading into the various science labs aboard ship, and is also affixed to all unsecured analytical devices within (such as portable microscopes and dissection equipment); it also can be found beside the doors to the quarters of the ship's science officer and all science specialists aboard. The Engineering logo can be found not only on the doors and bulkheads within the engineering section, but also appears on power supply trunk access plates and at coolant supply feed junctions, among other places.

Other graphics labels designate areas of the ship where extraordinary caution is required of personnel. Toxic gas, radiation, and thermowave hazard areas are all clearly marked, as are containers storing flammable or implosive materials.

Cargo labels are affixed to each of the cargo modules contained in the storage facility on R and S Decks. These markings indicate the origin and destination of each module, whether or not a stasis field is in use within, the assigned location within the cargo deck, the manifest code, and the category to which the contents belong.

Special labels are provided for medical cultures and lab specimens, including those to be refrigerated.

Other symbols serve as a directory to guide crew members to their destinations. Turbo elevator locations are pointed out along the ship's corridors, as are airlocks and spacesuit lockers. Graphics on the rec deck bulkheads point out various electronic games, and mark the vessel's bowling alley and racquetball court.

DOOR INSIGNIA

EXECUTIVE
SCIENCE OFFICER

CHIEF ENGINEER

DEPARTMENTAL LOGOS

COMMAND

SCIENCE

MEDICAL

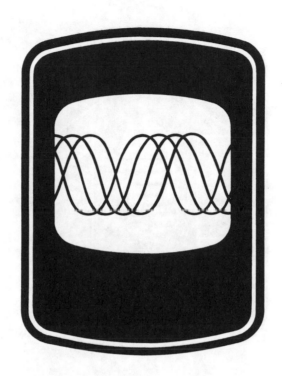

COMMUNICATIONS

ENGINEERING AND RELATED SERVICES

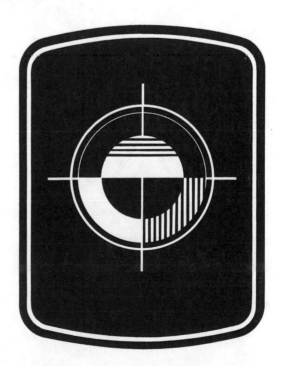

WEAPONS AND DEFENSE

TRANSPORTER SYSTEMS

SHIPBOARD SERVICES

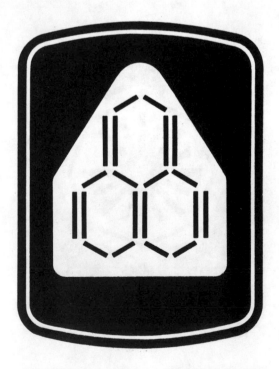

ENVIRONMENTAL ENGINEERING

SHIPBOARD SYMBOLS

DIRECTORY

REC DECK

TURBOLIFT

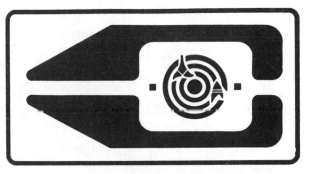

PHASER BATTLE GAMES

AIRLOCK/DOCKING PORT

THREE-DIMENSIONAL CHESS

CARGO FACILITY

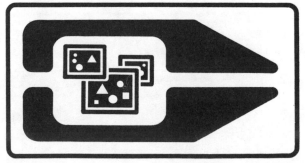

LIGHT CUBE TABLES

SHIP'S LAYOUT

A Deck is primarily composed of the vessel's main bridge, and it is from here that the commanding officer supervises the entire ship's operation. When seated in the command chair, located in the sunken center section, the commander has visual access to all major personnel stations and viewscreens, facilitating the decision-making process. This room is the nerve center of Enterprise, and is manned by the top officers of each department.

Navigation and vessel course control are carried out at the helm console, located in the center of the room. Directly above this station, affixed to the ceiling, is the navigational sensor input system. This device transmits by laser all input from the ship's main navigational sensor array [the dome above A Deck], and ties directly into the astrogator console beneath it.

Other stations are provided for communications, engineering, weapons control, gravity control, damage control, environmental engineering, sciences and library computer, and internal security. All stations are normally manned at all times.

The sciences station features two additional roll-out consoles. These are normally stored behind the station bulkhead, and both extend and retract automatically when activated by a switch on the center console.

Mounted into the room's forward bulkhead, on the ship's centerline, is the main viewing screen. This display produces a three-dimensional image, upon which computer graphics [also three-dimensional] may be super-imposed. Visual sensor pickups, located at various points on Enterprise's outer hull, are capable of image magnification and allow a varied choice of viewing angles.

Two turbolifts service the bridge. These shafts meet on B Deck and merge into a single vertical shaft which drops at the ship's centerline. The port-side turbolift is capable of rotating to give access to the A Deck airlock and docking port.

To protect against system failure or deliberate sabotage, A Deck features independent backup systems for battery power, gravity, and life support. These units activate automatically in the event of main system cutoff.

Located in the airlock/turbolift foyer is an automatic security scan system. This array, computer-controlled, prohibits any unauthorized or unaccompanied personnel from entering the bridge or the turbolift system.

Located in the floor, just forward of the helm console, is an emergency hatch to B Deck. This is provided for use in the event of turbolift failure.

The sciences station on the main bridge

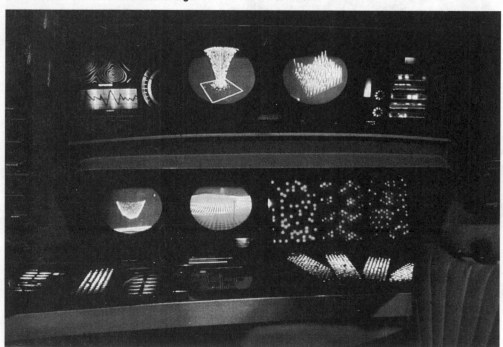

1 COMMUNICATIONS
2 ENGINEERING
3 WEAPONS AND DEFENSE
4 MAIN VIEWING SCREEN
5 GRAVITY CONTROL
6 DAMAGE AND REPAIR
7 ENVIRONMENTAL ENGINEERING
8 SCIENCES AND LIBRARY COMPUTER
9 INTERNAL SECURITY
10 COMMANDING OFFICER
11 NAVIGATOR
12 HELMSMAN

MAIN BRIDGE

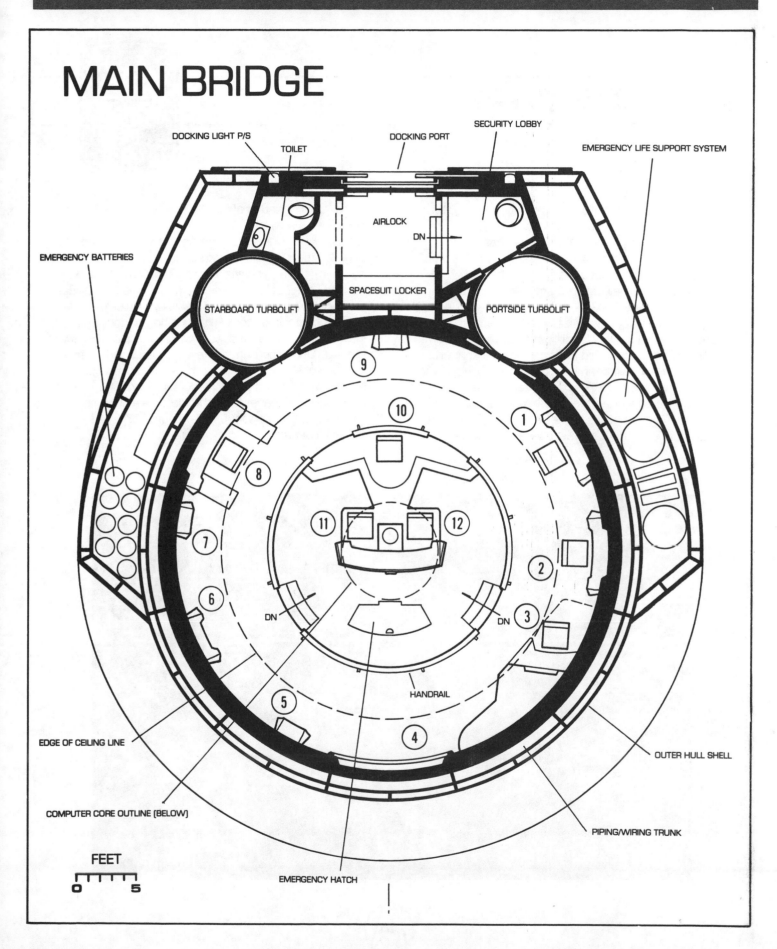

DOCKING LIGHT P/S

TOILET

DOCKING PORT

SECURITY LOBBY

EMERGENCY LIFE SUPPORT SYSTEM

AIRLOCK

DN

EMERGENCY BATTERIES

SPACESUIT LOCKER

STARBOARD TURBOLIFT

PORTSIDE TURBOLIFT

9

10

1

8

11

12

7

2

6

3

DN

DN

HANDRAIL

5

4

EDGE OF CEILING LINE

OUTER HULL SHELL

COMPUTER CORE OUTLINE (BELOW)

PIPING/WIRING TRUNK

FEET

0   5

EMERGENCY HATCH

DOCKING PORT

Star Fleet's standardized docking port system, introduced in 2211, was developed by Chiokis Starship Construction Corporation. This system, now in use on all Federation major vessels and shuttlecraft, was designed to free large hangar decks from V.I.P., personnel, and small cargo transfers, the frequency of which greatly taxed the lifespans of hangar pressurization/depressurization systems. Using these additional docking facilities, supply layover time has been greatly reduced and boarding personnel can now reach their shipboard destinations more quickly.

Externally, each docking port features a refueling system for Federation travel pods and shuttlecraft. Fuel transfer connectors meet automatically when a vessel docks, and fueling is controlled either from within the docked craft or by a wall panel within the host vessel's airlock.

EVA handgrips and docking lights surround the exterior port. Also provided is a power system patch-in which provides energy for equipment used outside the ship; this connector also provides recharge power for shuttle battery systems.

An auto-dock system surrounding the docking port insures first-time success when mating the two vessels. Once the ring latches are securely fastened, a door-grabber mechanism within Enterprise's bulkhead pulls the shuttle doors open and into a matching wallspace. The shuttle doors then remain within the Enterprise bulkhead until the vessel is ready to depart.

Starboard secondary hull--note docking ports

CONTRACTORS' SKETCHES

This main gangway design was adopted by
Star Fleet in 2213.
[Sketch courtesy of Chiokis
Starship Construction Corp.]

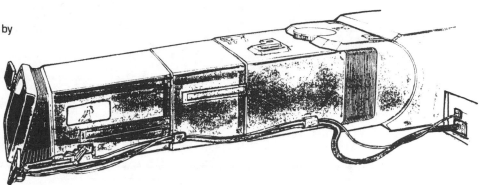

Star Fleet's standard docking system evolved
from these early concepts. [Sketch courtesy of
Chiokis Starship Construction Corp.]

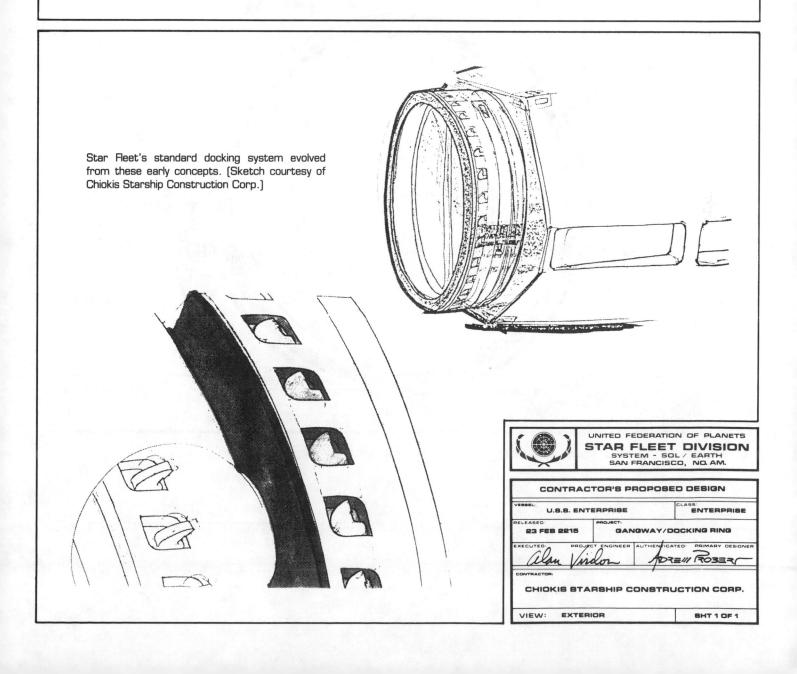

UNITED FEDERATION OF PLANETS
STAR FLEET DIVISION
SYSTEM - SOL / EARTH
SAN FRANCISCO, NO. AM.

CONTRACTOR'S PROPOSED DESIGN

VESSEL:	CLASS:
U.S.S. ENTERPRISE	**ENTERPRISE**

RELEASED:	PROJECT:
23 FEB 2215	**GANGWAY/DOCKING RING**

EXECUTED: PROJECT ENGINEER	AUTHENTICATED: PRIMARY DESIGNER
Alan Virdon	*Andrew Probert*

CONTRACTOR:

CHIOKIS STARSHIP CONSTRUCTION CORP.

VIEW: EXTERIOR	SHT 1 OF 1

DOCKING PORT

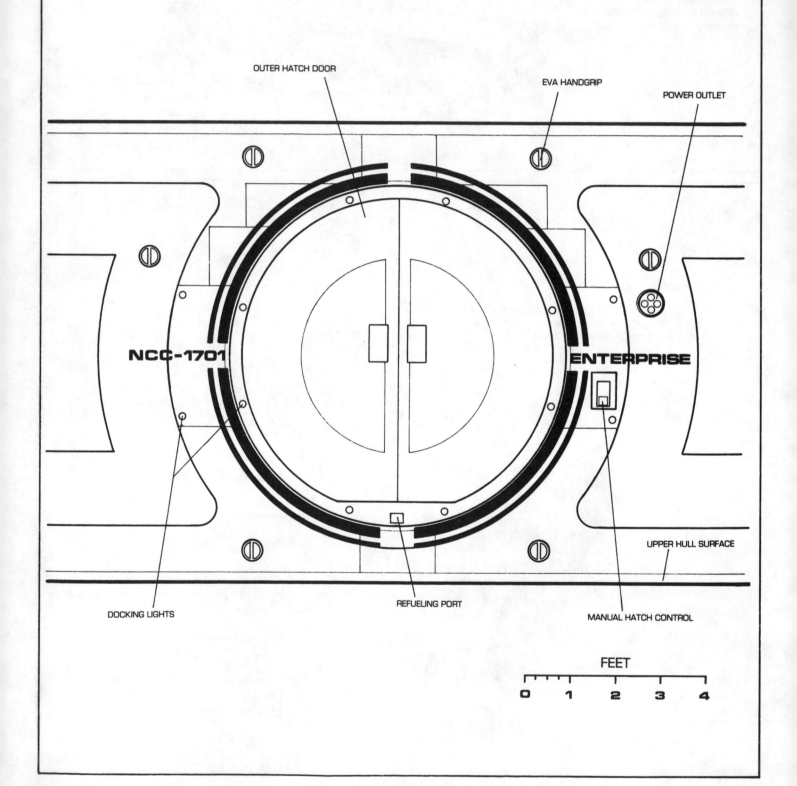

OUTER HATCH DOOR

EVA HANDGRIP

POWER OUTLET

NCC-1701

ENTERPRISE

DOCKING LIGHTS

REFUELING PORT

MANUAL HATCH CONTROL

UPPER HULL SURFACE

FEET

0   1   2   3   4

DOCKING PORT [SECTION]

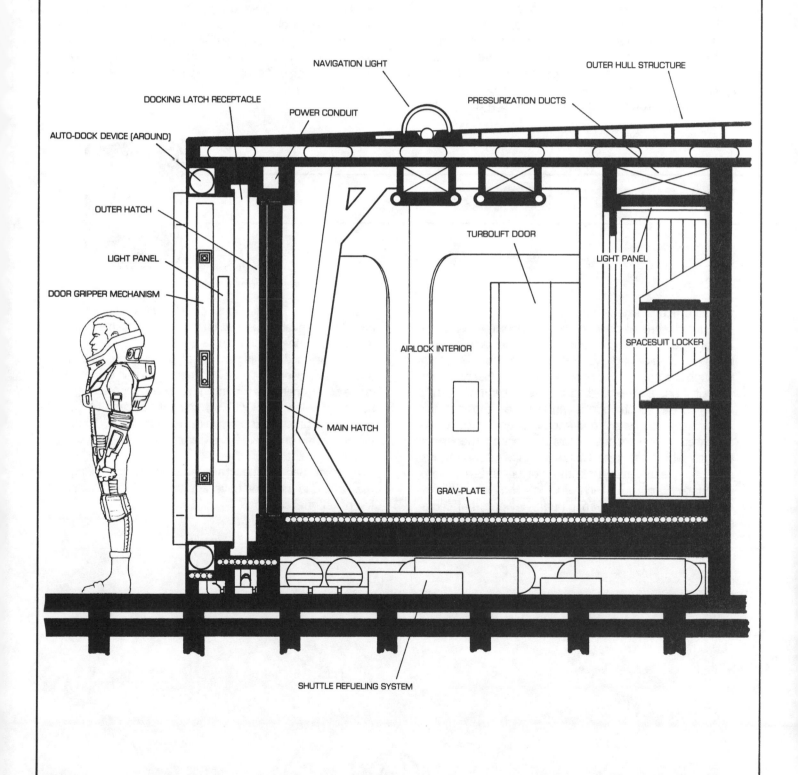

NAVIGATION LIGHT

OUTER HULL STRUCTURE

DOCKING LATCH RECEPTACLE

PRESSURIZATION DUCTS

POWER CONDUIT

AUTO-DOCK DEVICE [AROUND]

OUTER HATCH

TURBOLIFT DOOR

LIGHT PANEL

LIGHT PANEL

DOOR GRIPPER MECHANISM

SPACESUIT LOCKER

AIRLOCK INTERIOR

MAIN HATCH

GRAV-PLATE

SHUTTLE REFUELING SYSTEM

B Deck is generally utilized as a temporary holding area for persons, under incarceration, who have just entered or are preparing to leave the ship. Those to be held aboard ship for more than six hours are transferred to the main brig on G Deck; those departing Enterprise within three hours are transferred from the main brig to B Deck.

B Deck is the main security level. The Security Chief's office is located here, as are a break room and several small holding cells. A ladder leading down from the A Deck emergency hatch is mounted against the forward side of the central computer core, which stands in the middle of the deck. The level's forward bulkhead holds a door which leads to the top level of the ship's primary hull stairwell.

A special autolock device in the elevator door prevents unauthorized entry. An automatic security scan system warns of any unauthorized weaponry or personnel within the B Deck turbolift as it approaches, giving security personnel time to react should the autolock device be overriden.

Force field barriers seal the holding cells. These fields, impervious to hand-held weaponry, have backup power units which snap on if the main power circuitry fails.

V.I.P. FACILITIES

The officers' mess comprises most of C Deck. The donut-shaped central area, approximately equal in diameter to the main bridge, is a specialty kitchen capable of serving V.I.P.s cuisine not available through the ship's food processor units. Surrounding the kitchen, and extending to the outer hull, is the dining area; both booth and table seating are accessible, as are six food and beverage units. Wall-mounted viewscreens provide three-dimensional images which simulate windows; these screens are also capable of displaying movies or communications.

Located at the stern end of the level is the officers' lounge. Here, four huge viewports afford a spectacular view of the ship's warp nacelles and space beyond. To the sides, small planter areas hold flora from several Federation worlds and a small pool features fresh-water tropical fish.

Just forward of this section of the lounge is a bar and privacy area. Two viewscreens, similar to those in the dining area, are mounted into the lounge's stern bulkhead, allowing all V.I.P.'s immediate access to the full range of ship's communication services. These screens also provide a full exterior and interior tour of the vessel.

A snack bar on the starboard side of the lounge features one food and beverage unit, with two tables for personnel seating.

V.I.P. (OFFICERS') LOUNGE

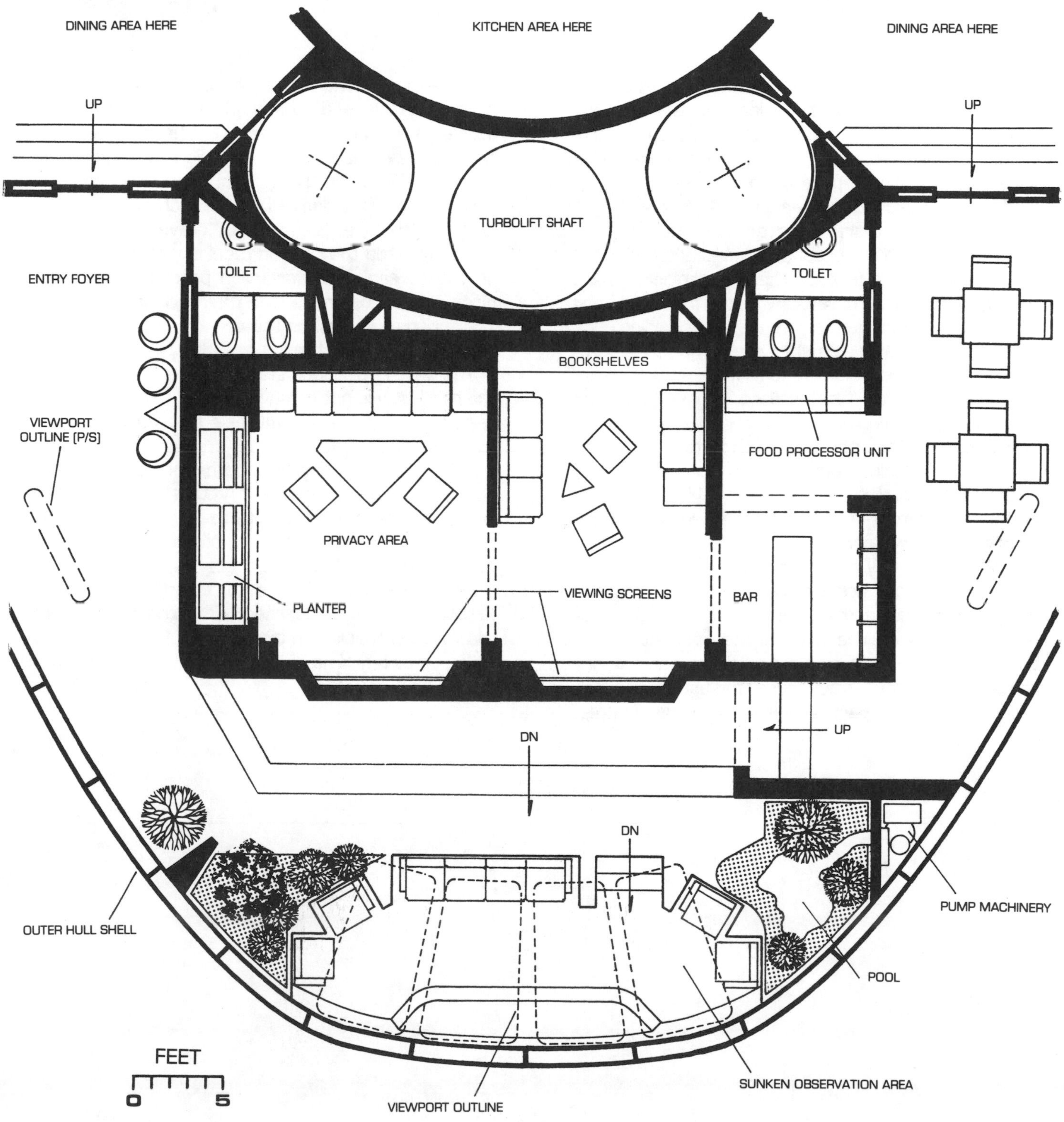

DINING AREA HERE

KITCHEN AREA HERE

DINING AREA HERE

UP

UP

TURBOLIFT SHAFT

ENTRY FOYER

TOILET

TOILET

BOOKSHELVES

FOOD PROCESSOR UNIT

VIEWPORT
OUTLINE (P/S)

PRIVACY AREA

PLANTER

VIEWING SCREENS

BAR

DN

UP

DN

OUTER HULL SHELL

PUMP MACHINERY

POOL

FEET

0   5

VIEWPORT OUTLINE

SUNKEN OBSERVATION AREA

MEAL SERVICE

Nutritech Corporation's new food processor system delivers exquisite cuisine with a speed and power efficiency never before possible. Unlike Enterprise's old food delivery system, which utilized mini-turbolifts which ran parallel to the main elevator system, the Nutritech design makes use of the latest in micro-transporter technology. All foodstuffs and beverages are manufactured on G Deck by the ship's food synthesis machinery, which draws basic protein, carbohydrate, fat, fiber, and other nutrient supplies from a series of holding units nearby. These basic elements are combined to form foods with flavors, colors, and textures which are indistinguishable from fresh meats, vegetables, fruits and grains. Beverages are also created in this manner. Finished items, complete with plates, trays, and glasses to contain them, are then transported by closed-circuit to the processor at which the order was placed. Order-to-delivery time can range from twenty to ninety seconds, depending upon the complexity and quantity of the order.

To use the food processor, one first calls up the menu display using the controls to the right. The menu, along with the appropriate request codes, then appears on the unit's display screen. At any point, as the menu list advances, the user may punch in the code for any particular item or group of items.

A three-dimensional image of the chosen meal then appears in place of the menu list on the display screen. If the user chooses, he or she may then continue to view the menu by touching the "menu advance" selector on the control panel. This process continues until the desired cuisine is chosen. To place an order, the user presses the "deliver" selector on the panel while the desired meal is visually displayed on the screen. The words "in process" appear in place of the food image, and the readout changes to "selection ready" when the order has been beamed to the processor's holding bin.

The holding bin door slides open automatically. If the meal tray is not removed within one minute, it is returned to the food synthesis unit and is broken down for later use.

When the user has finished his or her meal, the discarded tray, dinnerware, and trash are deposited into their appropriate receptacles on the front of the processor. These items are broken down, to be resynthesized and used at a later time.

All of the best menus of the thousand best restaurants in the Federation are programmed into the food synthesis computer. Any of these may be called up at any time. A partial menu listing appears on the opposite page.

FOOD PROCESSOR UNIT

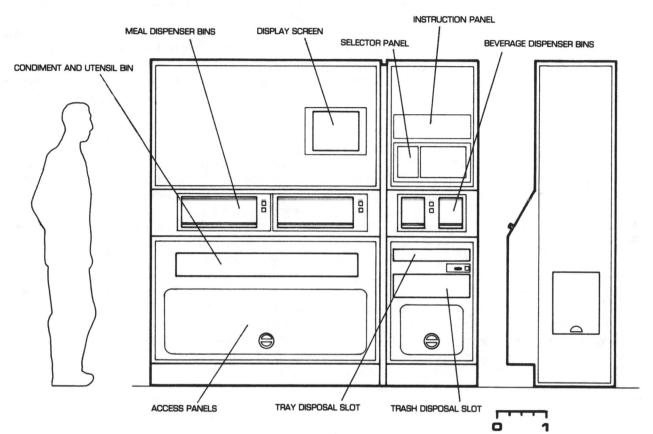

INSTRUCTION PANEL

MEAL DISPENSER BINS   DISPLAY SCREEN

SELECTOR PANEL   BEVERAGE DISPENSER BINS

CONDIMENT AND UTENSIL BIN

ACCESS PANELS   TRAY DISPOSAL SLOT   TRASH DISPOSAL SLOT

0   1

PARTIAL MENU LISTING

TERRAN

ASPARAGUS WITH BASIL SOUR CREAM
BAKED ACORN SQUASH
BARBECUED CHICKEN
BAVARIAN BRATWURST CASSEROLE
BEEF
   CHILI CON CARNE
   BEEF STROGANOFF
   SIRLOIN W/ BLUE RIBBON SAUCE
   YANKEE POT ROAST
BROCCOLI CASSEROLE
BURGUNDY BEEF
CARIBBEAN STEAK KABOBS
CHICKEN
   CHICKEN A LA KING
   ALMOND CHICKEN
   ASPARAGUS CHICKEN W/ BLACK BEAN SAUCE
   CHICKEN CACCIATORE
   CASHEW CHICKEN
   HAWAIIAN CHICKEN
CLAM CHOWDER
CORNISH HEN, LIME-GLAZED
DEVILED CRAB
DUCKLING W/ CHERRY SAUCE

EGGS BENEDICT
GERMAN POTATO SALAD
HAM W/ PINEAPPLE
LAMB CHOPS A L'ORANGE
LOBSTER TAILS
MACARONI AND CHEESE
MUSHROOM-CHEESE CANAPES
NUTS (ASSORTED)
ORIENTAL BROWN RICE
OYSTERS (SCALLOPED)
PERCH W/ DILL
PORK, SWEET AND SOUR
POTATOES AU GRATIN
PUMPKIN PIE
RATATOUILLE
SOUFFLE, CHEESE
STUFFED PORK CHOPS
TROUT AMANDINE W/ PINEAPPLE
VEAL PARMESAN
ZUCCHINI PROVENCALE

VULCAN

ADRONN FELTARA
B'LLTARR

BERTAKK SOUP
C'TORR
FILRAK
FARR-KAHLI
IHNTYA
KAHRI-TORRAFEIACA
KLEETANTA W/ FORATI SAUCE
L-LERSA
MIA-ZED
PLOMEEK SOUP
T'CORACA

ANDORIAN

AKHARRAD
ALARDI PARTINNA
DREAAK
DUUPLONI
HONAR
NECREENA
SKOPAR
SOHLA T'POCOWAN
YUTANN

D Deck houses the ship's V.I.P. staterooms. These compartments serve as quarters for visiting officers, ambassadors and their wives or husbands, and Federation government officials, among others. Each stateroom is composed of two areas which are separated by a retractable, transparent aluminum partition. The room's entrance opens into the sleeping area, which has two beds. A transparent door leads into the bathroom area, which features both a sonic shower and a jacuzzi tub. Here, also, is a clothes closet.

The other half of the stateroom is a work area. A library computer terminal and work desk are provided for guest use, for which instructions are provided. A circular dining booth is provided for those guests who prefer to eat alone or who desire to work during their meal.

A viewscreen station stands against one wall. Here, guests may contact their home worlds by subspace radio, if necessary, or they may simply choose from thousands of entertainment movies or sports events as they desire.

A small storage closet is provided for those with luggage or small personal cargo which cannot be stored away on the cargo deck.

For convienience, the stateroom foyer contains a wall-mounted food processor unit. This processor, a Nutritech design, is smaller than those used in public areas of the ship but its function is essentially the same.

Personal items may be stored on a bookshelf above the beds, or in a set of roll-top cabinets on the work area wall.

Also on D Deck are a conference room, where closed meetings may be held, and the ship's junior officers' quarters.

Water tanks and pump machinery ring the periphery of the deck, behind the outer bulkheads. Housed in this area also, at bow, port, and starboard positions, are Enterprise's upper phaser banks.

Keeping with Star Fleet tradition, E Deck houses the senior officers' quarters. These staterooms are quite similar to the V.I.P. units on D Deck, with only a few differences.

The sleeping area holds a single large bed which can double as a sofa during off-duty relaxation.

The room's corner circular nook, normally occupied by a dining booth, can be modified at the officer's request before leaving drydock. Several corner modules are available, including a lighted display alcove, an electronic game booth, a personal workout machine, an altar platform for personal religious use, and a hobbycraft work area, among others.

V.I.P. STATEROOM

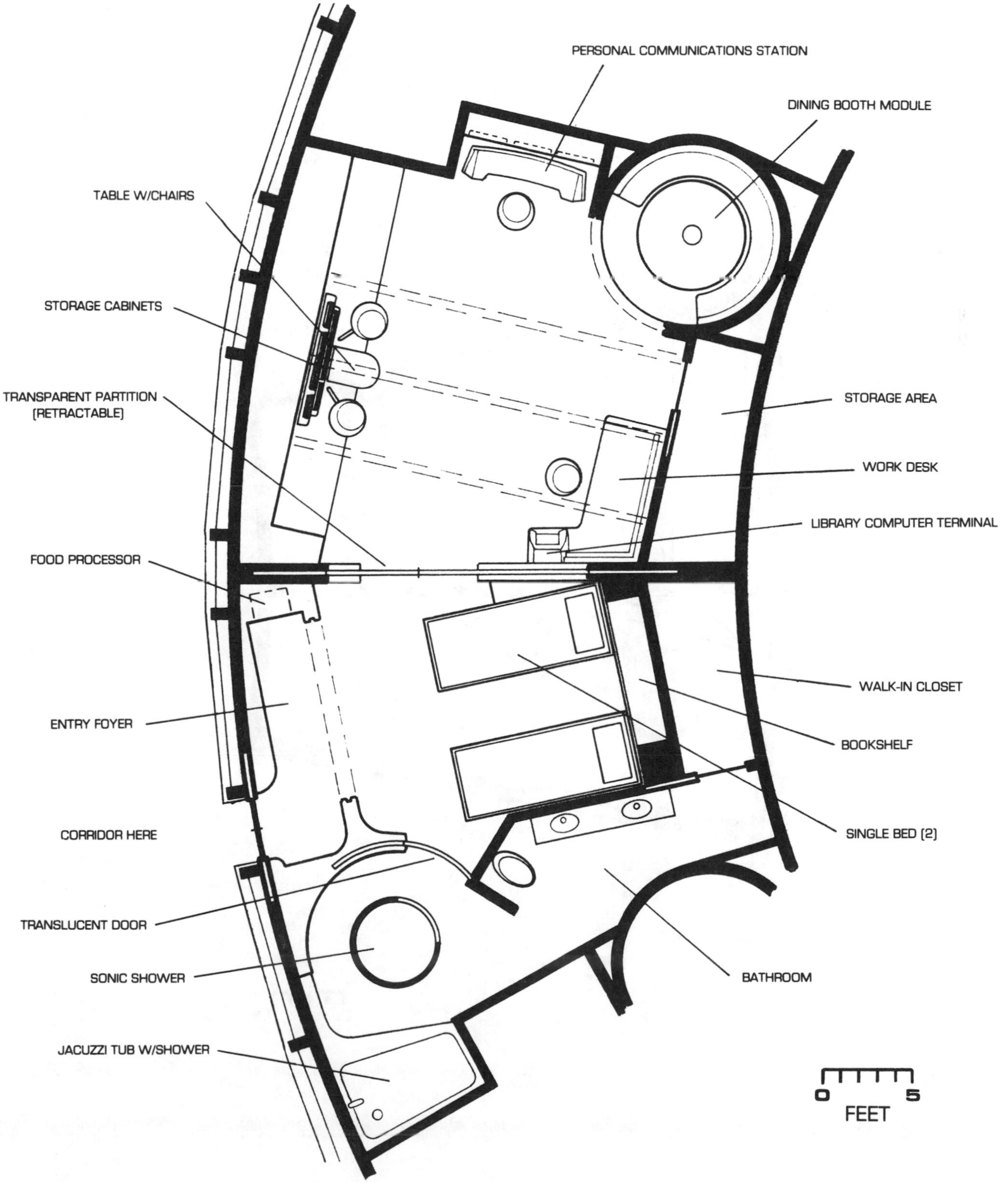

PERSONAL COMMUNICATIONS STATION

DINING BOOTH MODULE

TABLE W/CHAIRS

STORAGE CABINETS

TRANSPARENT PARTITION
[RETRACTABLE]

STORAGE AREA

WORK DESK

LIBRARY COMPUTER TERMINAL

FOOD PROCESSOR

ENTRY FOYER

WALK-IN CLOSET

BOOKSHELF

CORRIDOR HERE

SINGLE BED (2)

TRANSLUCENT DOOR

SONIC SHOWER

BATHROOM

JACUZZI TUB W/SHOWER

0   5
FEET

JUNIOR OFFICERS' QUARTERS

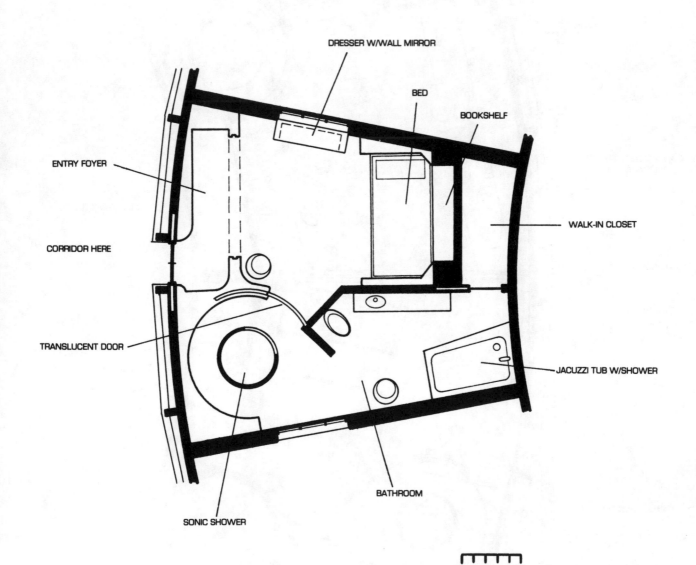

DRESSER W/WALL MIRROR

BED

BOOKSHELF

ENTRY FOYER

WALK-IN CLOSET

CORRIDOR HERE

TRANSLUCENT DOOR

JACUZZI TUB W/SHOWER

BATHROOM

SONIC SHOWER

0   5
FEET

SENIOR OFFICERS' QUARTERS

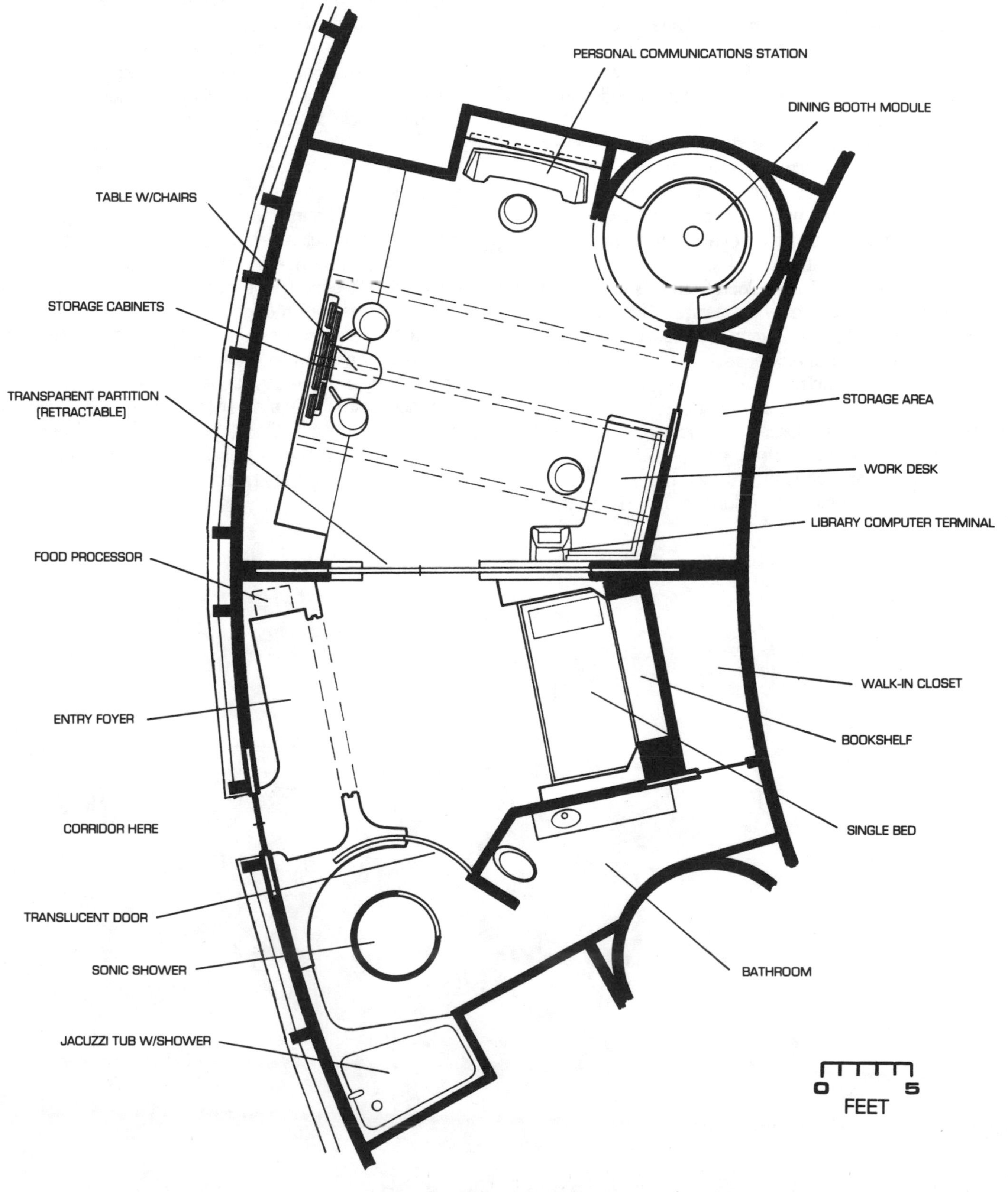

PERSONAL COMMUNICATIONS STATION

DINING BOOTH MODULE

TABLE W/CHAIRS

STORAGE CABINETS

TRANSPARENT PARTITION
(RETRACTABLE)

STORAGE AREA

WORK DESK

LIBRARY COMPUTER TERMINAL

FOOD PROCESSOR

ENTRY FOYER

WALK-IN CLOSET

BOOKSHELF

SINGLE BED

CORRIDOR HERE

TRANSLUCENT DOOR

SONIC SHOWER

BATHROOM

JACUZZI TUB W/SHOWER

0   5
FEET

The majority of F Deck is occupied by crew's quarters. These staterooms are structured as double suites, with private sleeping areas sharing a common, central bathroom. A three-drawer dresser/wall mirror unit is mounted near the bed, as in the junior officers' quarters. Crew members are invited to decorate their staterooms in whatever manner they wish, so long as Star Fleet standards of decorum are met.

The crew's messrooms are located in the center of the deck. These are open continuously, as the crew operates in three shifts around the clock and usually eat when they please. Those who wish to do so may eat in their rooms or even at their duty stations, if their workload allows.

Adjoining the rec deck balcony, on the starboard rear quarter, is the crew's lounge. This room is similar to the officer's lounge and features a bar, viewscreens, and a snack area.

On the aft centerline of F Deck is the impulse engineering section. This area is similar in layout to warp engineering on O Deck, but has additional parts shops and a standby engineering computer system to be used in the event of primary hull separation. The massive impulse deflection crystal dominates the upper center of the room, throwing a display of light patterns across the compartment. Energy carrier shafts connect the crystal to the impulse engines, which translate the intermix power into forward thrust for the vessel.

Five large fusion reactors are mounted between the impulse engines. Should hull separation occur, these furnaces take the place of the intermix system and drive their combined energies into the deflection crystal. In the unlikely event of a reactor failure, overload, or meltdown, the five fusion units are independently ejectable from the ship.

An elevator maintenance shop is located just forward of the impulse deck.

Personnel hatch airlocks are located at various points on F Deck. These rooms allow direct access to the primary hull's upper surface by utilizing small lift platforms which rise until flush with the outer hull.

Gangway access to Enterprise while in drydock is provided by a special hatch on the saucer rim, at the port centerline. This main hatchway, by ramp, allows direct entry into F Deck, and crew members are urged to board the ship in this manner whenever possible. This hatch is provided with a small airlock, though it is not normally used for EVA purposes.

CREW'S QUARTERS

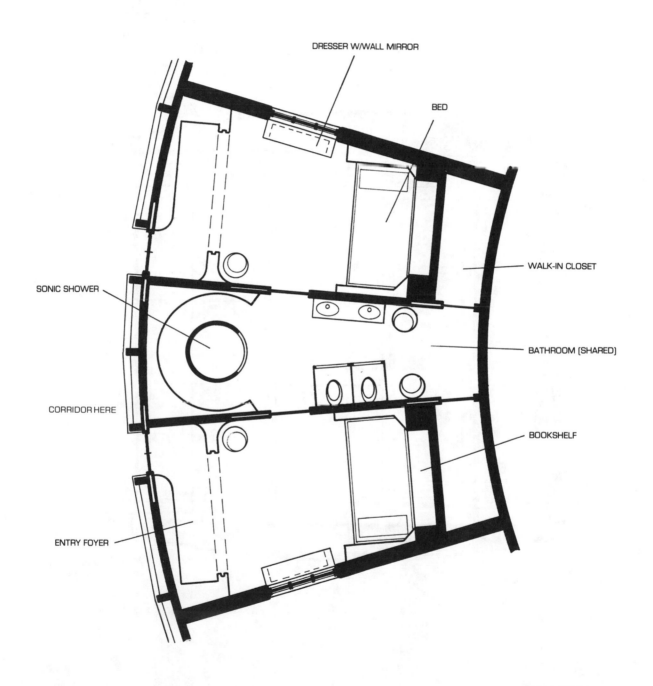

DRESSER W/WALL MIRROR

BED

WALK-IN CLOSET

SONIC SHOWER

BATHROOM [SHARED]

CORRIDOR HERE

BOOKSHELF

ENTRY FOYER

0   5
FEET

TURBOLIFT CAR

SECTION

ELEVATION

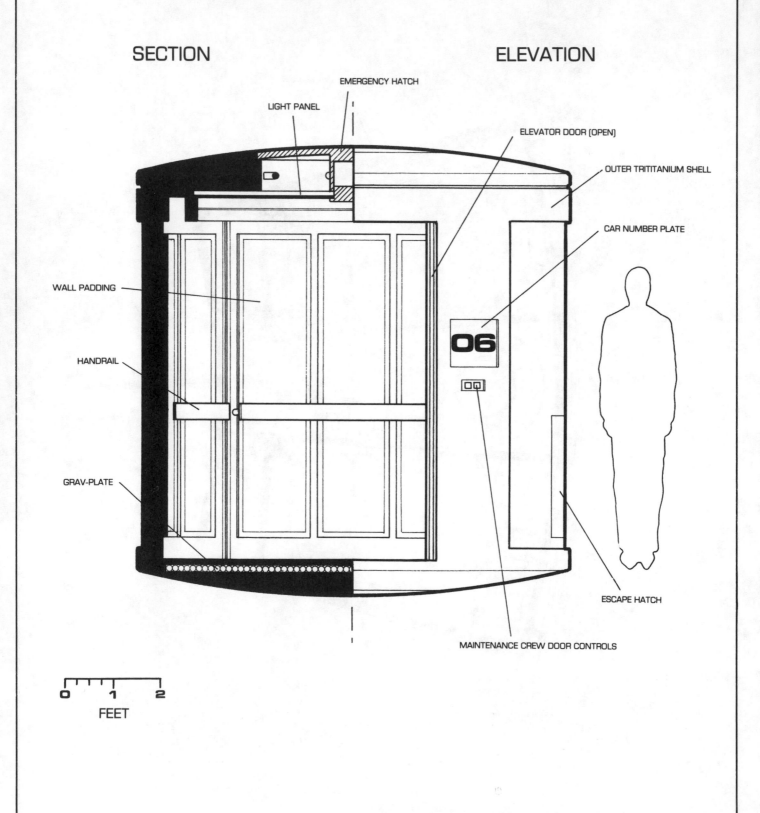

EMERGENCY HATCH

LIGHT PANEL

ELEVATOR DOOR (OPEN)

OUTER TRITITANIUM SHELL

CAR NUMBER PLATE

WALL PADDING

06

HANDRAIL

GRAV-PLATE

MAINTENANCE CREW DOOR CONTROLS

ESCAPE HATCH

0 1 2

FEET

PERSONNEL HATCH AIRLOCK

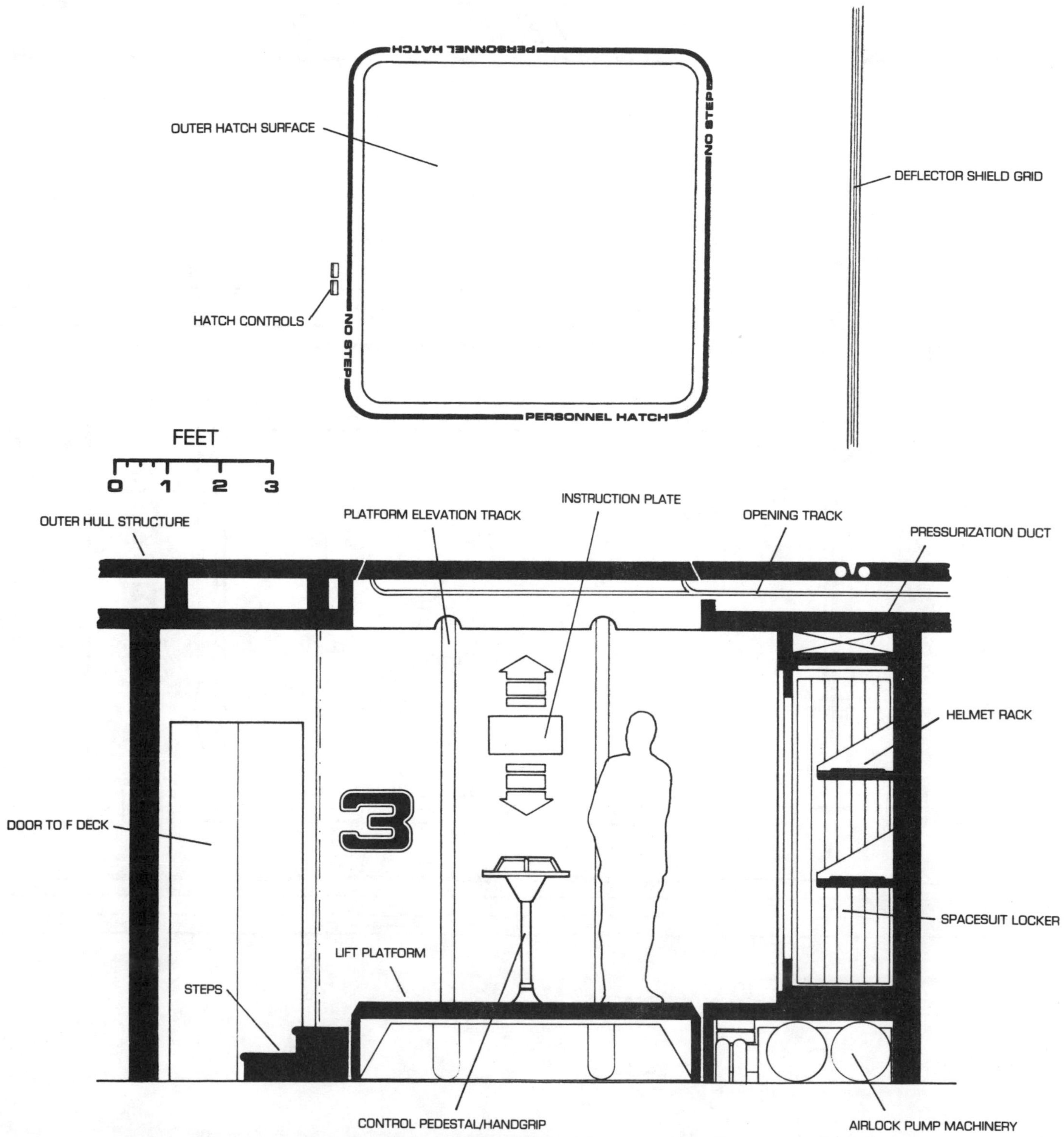

PERSONNEL HATCH

NO STEP

NO STEP

PERSONNEL HATCH

OUTER HATCH SURFACE

HATCH CONTROLS

DEFLECTOR SHIELD GRID

FEET

0 1 2 3

OUTER HULL STRUCTURE

PLATFORM ELEVATION TRACK

INSTRUCTION PLATE

OPENING TRACK

PRESSURIZATION DUCT

HELMET RACK

3

DOOR TO F DECK

SPACESUIT LOCKER

LIFT PLATFORM

STEPS

CONTROL PEDESTAL/HANDGRIP

AIRLOCK PUMP MACHINERY

MAIN GANGWAY HATCH

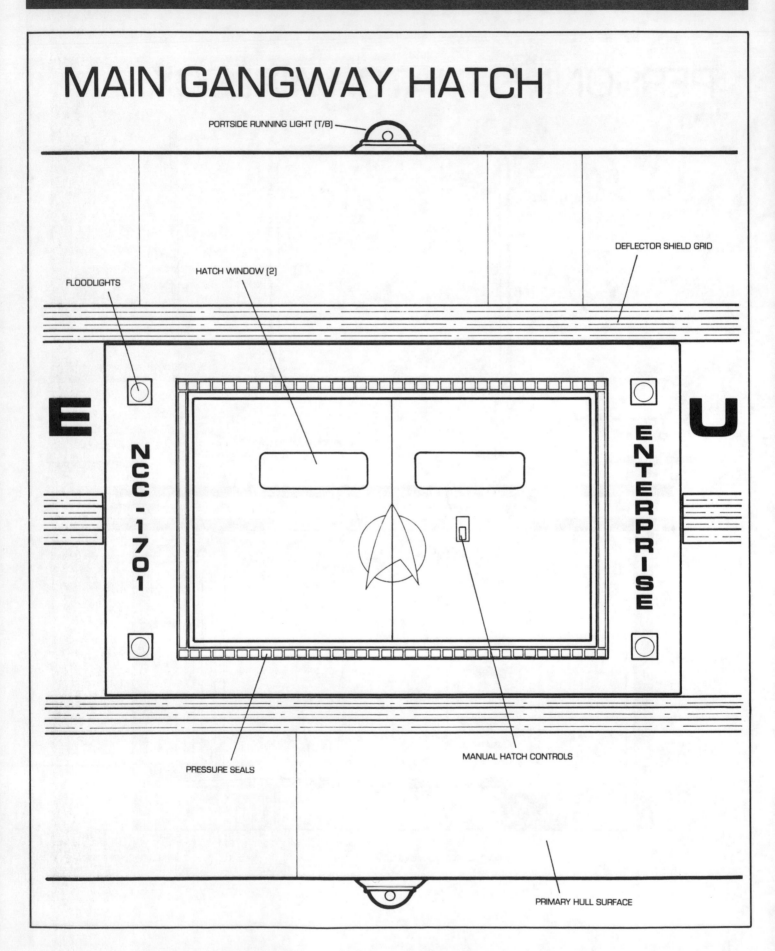

PORTSIDE RUNNING LIGHT [T/B]

DEFLECTOR SHIELD GRID

HATCH WINDOW [2]

FLOODLIGHTS

NCC-1701

ENTERPRISE

PRESSURE SEALS

MANUAL HATCH CONTROLS

PRIMARY HULL SURFACE

Often referred to as the "main deck," G Deck houses the majority of Enterprise's personnel support systems.

At the midpoint of the level, surrounding the computer core, is the ship's auxiliary control room. Sometimes called the "emergency bridge," this room assumes all functions of the main bridge should that A Deck primary fail. Normally unmanned, auxiliary control differs in configuration from the main bridge but all duty stations are present, as is a large main viewing screen. Designed for use in extreme combat situations, this room, deep within the primary hull, is the best protected aboard ship.

The improved sickbay complex forms an aft half-ring near the center of G Deck. All of the latest dovolopments in Federation medical technology are represented here, many of which were only theory a few years ago. New micro-diagnostic tables are capable of fully analyzing at the sub-cellular level all parts of the human body, affording the physician a total understanding of the patient's status. A closed-circuit mini-transporter system, installed at various locations throughout the medical section, allows tissue samples and cultures to be sent instantaneously to or from any lab aboard ship.

A new addition, utilized first in land-based Federation hospitals, is the medical stasis unit. In this room, patients whose conditions are considered immediately life-threatening can be placed into suspended animation until the proper cure or surgical procedure can be established. This unit is also used, if necessary, to stop the deterioration of a patient's condition until an outside medical facility can be reached. Use of the stasis unit takes place solely at the discretion of the attending surgeon or physician; cases where physical body damage is considered to be irreparable and terminal are not generally candidates for stasis, for the device is not intended for the prolongation of certain death.

The transporter rooms on this level have been rearranged somewhat. Those units previously located on level eight have been moved up one deck, and the majority of Enterprise's standard and emergency transporter rooms now form a centralized complex at G Deck's forward center. One transporter features a single, large pad (much like a cargo transporter) and adjoins and is devoted solely to the medical section; in this way, injured personnel on stretchers or who are otherwise lying prone may be beamed aboard.

Also on G Deck, near the transporter complex, is the main briefing room. It is used primarily by command and medical personnel for discussion purposes, but also serves as a debriefing facility for newly-returned landing parties. The briefing room features a large viewing screen which can be controlled either from a console at the screen's base or at the science officer's computer panel at the table.

Adjoining the briefing room is the ship's armory. Here, hand-held weaponry and other small arms are distributed for landing party or security use. This room is guarded at all times.

At the starboard rear is the two-level rec deck. This large room furnishes off-duty personnel with electronic games and library facilites, as well as a multi-screen display area which shows a pictorial history of Star Fleet and all earlier vessels named "Enterprise." Public relations events are held here, as are all political gatherings; for this reason, the rec deck restrooms are marked "male" and "female" in order to accomodate non-crew personnel. Bowling and racquetball facilities adjoin the rec deck on the starboard side.

The vessel's chapel is found on this level. Weekly services are held here by the ship's chaplain, as are weddings, funerals, and other customary gatherings.

Much of G Deck, in a wide area encircling the level, does not attain full ceiling height. This is due to the underside concave structure of the primary hull. This area houses cargo, the food synthesis system, the saucer's life support, air conditioning, and battery systems, pump machinery, port and starboard fresh water tanks, and the ship's sanitary wastes recovery unit.

It is also this area in which the Enterprise's four massive emergency landing legs are mounted. These units are stowed retracted, filling a bay which carries up to F Deck. Extension of the landing legs allows the primary hull to safely make planetfall following hull separation.

Science labs, the main brig, and the ship's gymnasium lie around the outer perimeter of G Deck.

AUXILIARY CONTROL ROOM

1 WEAPONS AND DEFENSE
2 ENGINEERING
3 MAIN VIEWING SCREEN
4 COMMUNICATIONS
5 HELMSMAN
6 NAVIGATOR
7 COMMANDING OFFICER
8 SCIENCES
9 M-6 MONITOR
10 M-6 OVERRIDE PANEL
11 ENVIRONMENTAL CONTROL
12 DAMAGE AND REPAIR
13 INTERNAL SECURITY
14 GRAVITY CONTROL

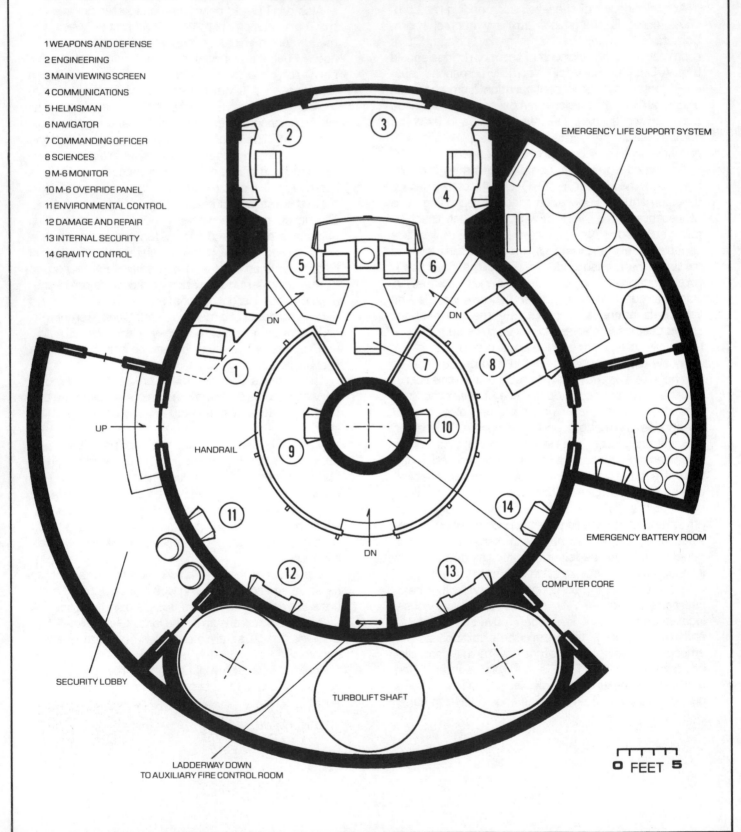

EMERGENCY LIFE SUPPORT SYSTEM

DN

DN

HANDRAIL

UP

EMERGENCY BATTERY ROOM

COMPUTER CORE

DN

SECURITY LOBBY

TURBOLIFT SHAFT

LADDERWAY DOWN
TO AUXILIARY FIRE CONTROL ROOM

0 FEET 5

CORRIDOR REDESIGN

In order to maximize the use of space aboard ship, the Enterprise corridor system has been designed to provide more than simply access from room to room. Several safety and survival features are built into its walls and ceilings.

The corridors are of two types: radial (those which run outward, pointing toward the outer hull) and concentric (those which lie in rings, interconnecting the radial corridors). The angled surfaces of each conceal different support structures.

Radial corridors are angled on either side. Their walls conceal a variety of supply lines and conduction systems, data networks, and power trunks. These systems are accessible by the removal of the snap-locked panels which cover them, and all are clearly marked.

The ship's concentric corridors house personnel support systems. In each corridor segment, there exists an emergency survival compartment which provides atmosphere, food, communications, and waste management facilities for one crew member; this provision is to be used should sudden decompression of the ship interior occur due to hull damage or life support failure. A zip-seal pressure bag folds up out of the compartment's padding, allowing the user to be transported to safety by spacesuited personnel.

Beneath the survival compartment, accessible by a separate wall panel, is a survival suit locker. These suits, more compact than standard spacesuits, slip on quickly and provide air and heat for two hours. Each locker contains two suits.

Above, near the ceiling, is an emergency equipment locker. Here can be found additional life support units for survival suits, cutting torches, emergency beacons, communicators, tether lines, and other equipment.

Each segment has, mounted to the ceiling, a personnel locator display. This unit shows the number and placement of persons in the adjoining corridor section.

The corridor panels on D, E, and G Decks are covered by a layer of padding to help protect against injury during any unlikely sudden ship movement.

The corridors on each deck are color-coded for easy identification of deck level. Colors are as follows: D, brown; E, red; F, silver; G, white; H, light blue; I, yellow. All secondary hull corridors are silver.

Concentric Corridor Section (note condition red tracer lights)

CONCENTRIC CORRIDOR
(SECTION A-A)

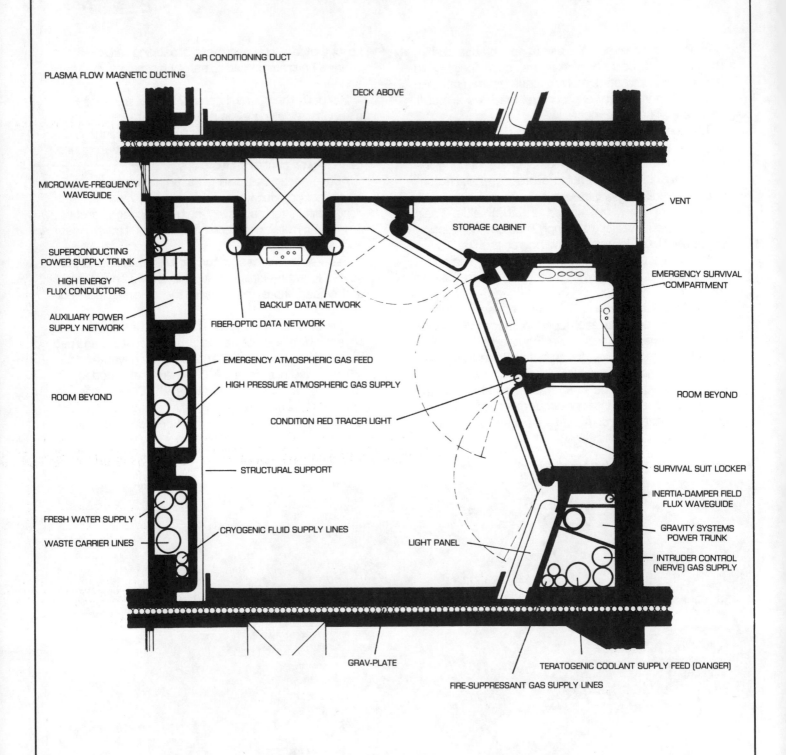

PLASMA FLOW MAGNETIC DUCTING

AIR CONDITIONING DUCT

DECK ABOVE

MICROWAVE-FREQUENCY WAVEGUIDE

VENT

STORAGE CABINET

SUPERCONDUCTING POWER SUPPLY TRUNK

HIGH ENERGY FLUX CONDUCTORS

EMERGENCY SURVIVAL COMPARTMENT

AUXILIARY POWER SUPPLY NETWORK

BACKUP DATA NETWORK

FIBER-OPTIC DATA NETWORK

EMERGENCY ATMOSPHERIC GAS FEED

HIGH PRESSURE ATMOSPHERIC GAS SUPPLY

ROOM BEYOND

ROOM BEYOND

CONDITION RED TRACER LIGHT

STRUCTURAL SUPPORT

SURVIVAL SUIT LOCKER

INERTIA-DAMPER FIELD FLUX WAVEGUIDE

FRESH WATER SUPPLY

CRYOGENIC FLUID SUPPLY LINES

GRAVITY SYSTEMS POWER TRUNK

WASTE CARRIER LINES

LIGHT PANEL

INTRUDER CONTROL (NERVE) GAS SUPPLY

GRAV-PLATE

TERATOGENIC COOLANT SUPPLY FEED (DANGER)

FIRE-SUPPRESSANT GAS SUPPLY LINES

CONCENTRIC CORRIDOR (ELEVATION)

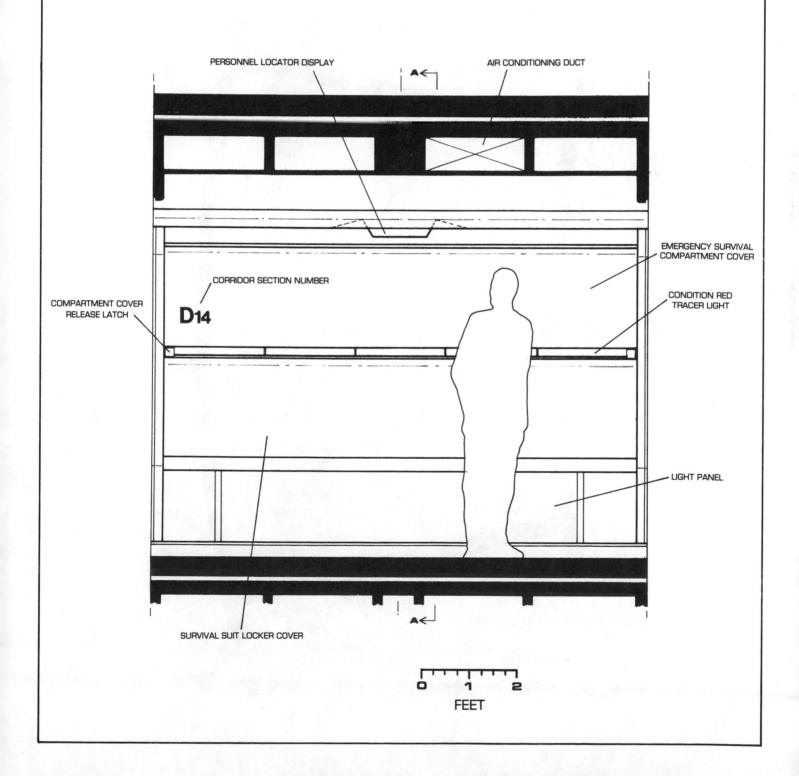

PERSONNEL LOCATOR DISPLAY

AIR CONDITIONING DUCT

EMERGENCY SURVIVAL
COMPARTMENT COVER

CORRIDOR SECTION NUMBER

D14

CONDITION RED
TRACER LIGHT

COMPARTMENT COVER
RELEASE LATCH

LIGHT PANEL

SURVIVAL SUIT LOCKER COVER

0   1   2
FEET

BRIEFING ROOM

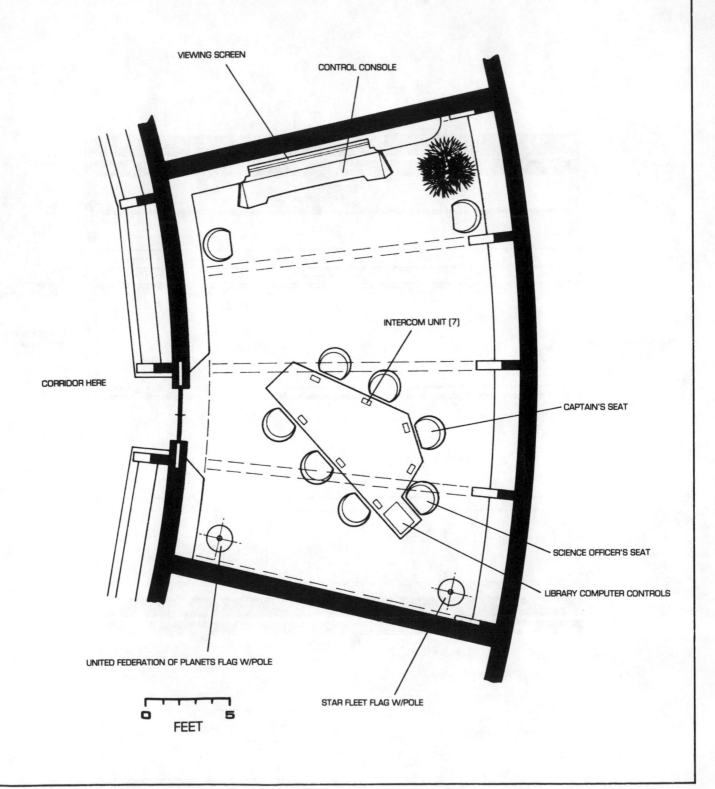

VIEWING SCREEN

CONTROL CONSOLE

INTERCOM UNIT (7)

CORRIDOR HERE

CAPTAIN'S SEAT

SCIENCE OFFICER'S SEAT

LIBRARY COMPUTER CONTROLS

UNITED FEDERATION OF PLANETS FLAG W/POLE

STAR FLEET FLAG W/POLE

0   5

FEET

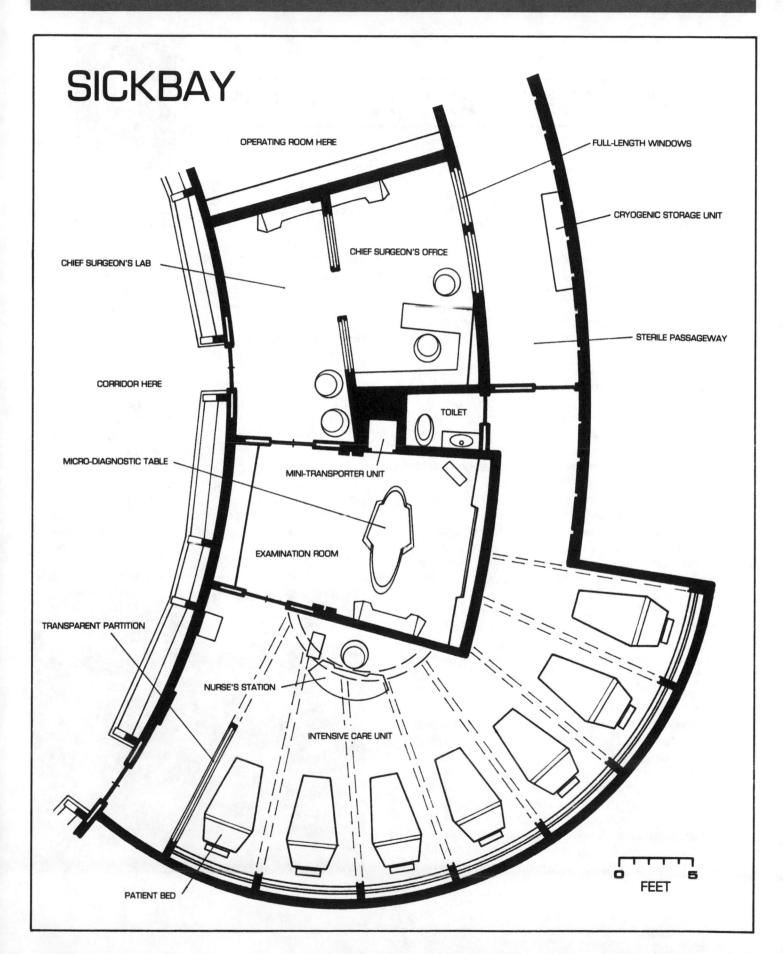

SICKBAY

OPERATING ROOM HERE

FULL-LENGTH WINDOWS

CRYOGENIC STORAGE UNIT

CHIEF SURGEON'S OFFICE

CHIEF SURGEON'S LAB

STERILE PASSAGEWAY

CORRIDOR HERE

TOILET

MICRO-DIAGNOSTIC TABLE

MINI-TRANSPORTER UNIT

EXAMINATION ROOM

TRANSPARENT PARTITION

NURSE'S STATION

INTENSIVE CARE UNIT

PATIENT BED

0 FEET 5

TRANSPORTERS/EQUIPMENT

The Enterprise transporter system is the result of more than nine years of intensive research and development, and is the most powerful yet efficient in use today. Safe beaming range has been increased from 16,000 to 19,500 miles, with a greater object-mass/beaming-distance ratio than in past models.

All transport system machinery is now housed within the floor of the room. This design allows for easy access when repair or adjustment is necessary, and frees up adjoining rooms for use as habitable space. Aluminum grate flooring provides access to the transport platform and control pod.

The transport platform features six pads, which are numbered clockwise, beginning with the right front. Pad number one is used when only one person is to beam to or from the ship. A redesigned field generator matrix is mounted into the rear wall of the chamber, which operates with less waste heat than was experienced in earlier configurations.

The transporter operator stands within an enclosed control pod, which has a floor-to-ceiling transparent aluminum panel through which he or she may view the transport platform. This panel serves to shield the operator from the effects of any cumulative radiations emitted by the new transporter machinery, a side effect of the more powerful system. Persons on the platform are protected by an invisible force field which automatically activates and functions until the end of the beaming process. Any such radiations are negligable, but could be harmful with prolonged exposure.

In the new system, transporter energies are transmitted and received from any of several transmission points on the outer hull. These points, less than two feet across, are protected by separate deflector shield units which allow beaming to take place while the remainder of the ship is fully protected. This feature is particularly valuable during combat situations.

A door in the standard transporter room wall leads to a staging area where landing parties prepare for transport. Four spacesuit lockers line one wall; each contains one suit, providing enough to clothe a standard party of four. A small, locked arms cabinet holds phasers, which must be registered and assigned before use. Communicators, tricorders, translators, and outerwear are contained in a separate cabinet on another wall.

Large double doors lead from the staging room into a twenty-two man transporter facility. This is reserved for emergency use, as when the crew must abandon ship.

There are four standard six-man transporters and four emergency platforms within the transport complex. One small cargo unit allows precious cargo to be beamed up from the secondary hull before emergency hull separation takes place.

The range of the standard communicator has been increased to twenty thousand miles. This device is an updated version of the flip-grid unit which has proven so successful. A wrist communicator was also utilized until recently, but repeated failures after relatively

Transporter room interior (viewed from platform)

TRANSPORTER ROOM

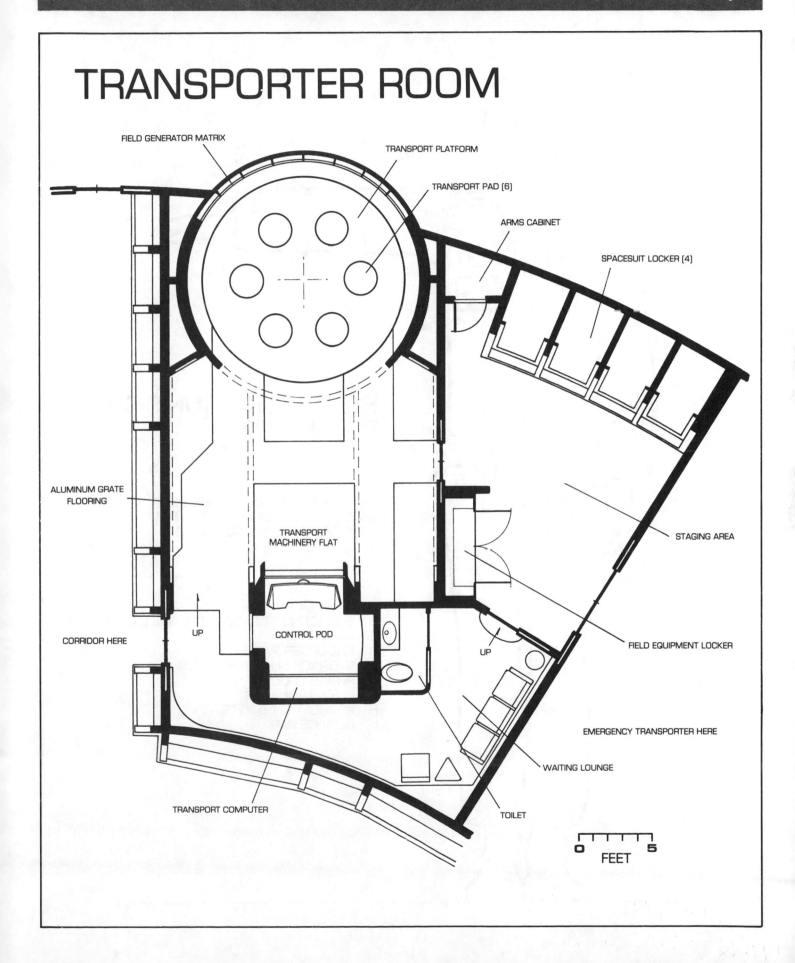

FIELD GENERATOR MATRIX

TRANSPORT PLATFORM

TRANSPORT PAD [6]

ARMS CABINET

SPACESUIT LOCKER [4]

ALUMINUM GRATE FLOORING

STAGING AREA

TRANSPORT MACHINERY FLAT

CORRIDOR HERE

UP

CONTROL POD

UP

FIELD EQUIPMENT LOCKER

EMERGENCY TRANSPORTER HERE

TRANSPORT COMPUTER

TOILET

WAITING LOUNGE

0   5
FEET

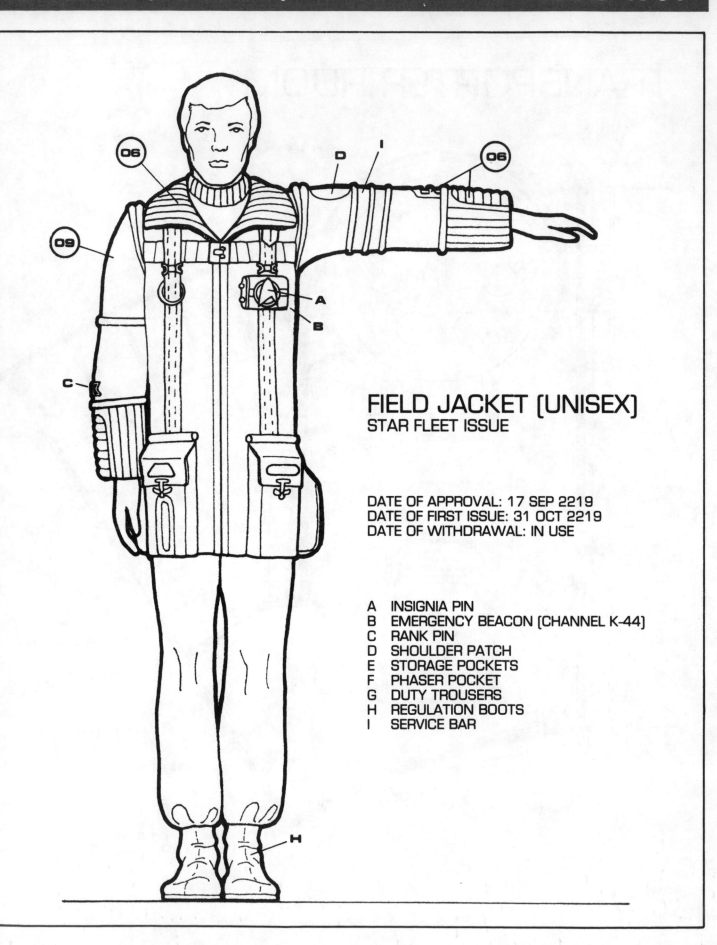

FIELD JACKET [UNISEX]
STAR FLEET ISSUE

DATE OF APPROVAL: 17 SEP 2219
DATE OF FIRST ISSUE: 31 OCT 2219
DATE OF WITHDRAWAL: IN USE

A   INSIGNIA PIN
B   EMERGENCY BEACON [CHANNEL K-44]
C   RANK PIN
D   SHOULDER PATCH
E   STORAGE POCKETS
F   PHASER POCKET
G   DUTY TROUSERS
H   REGULATION BOOTS
I   SERVICE BAR

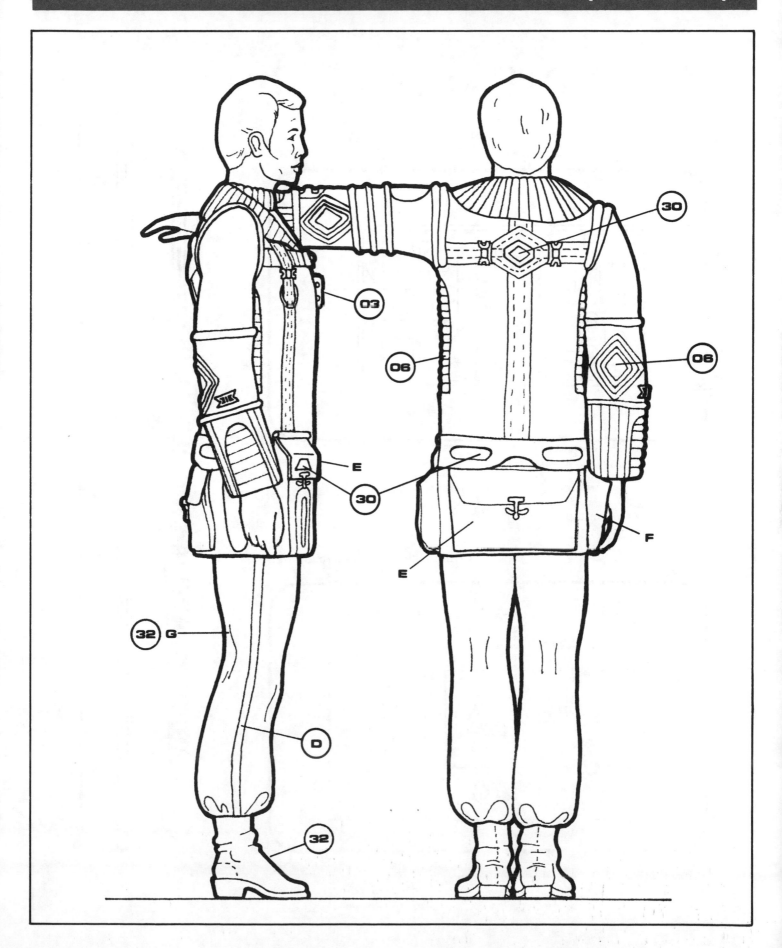

COMMUNICATOR

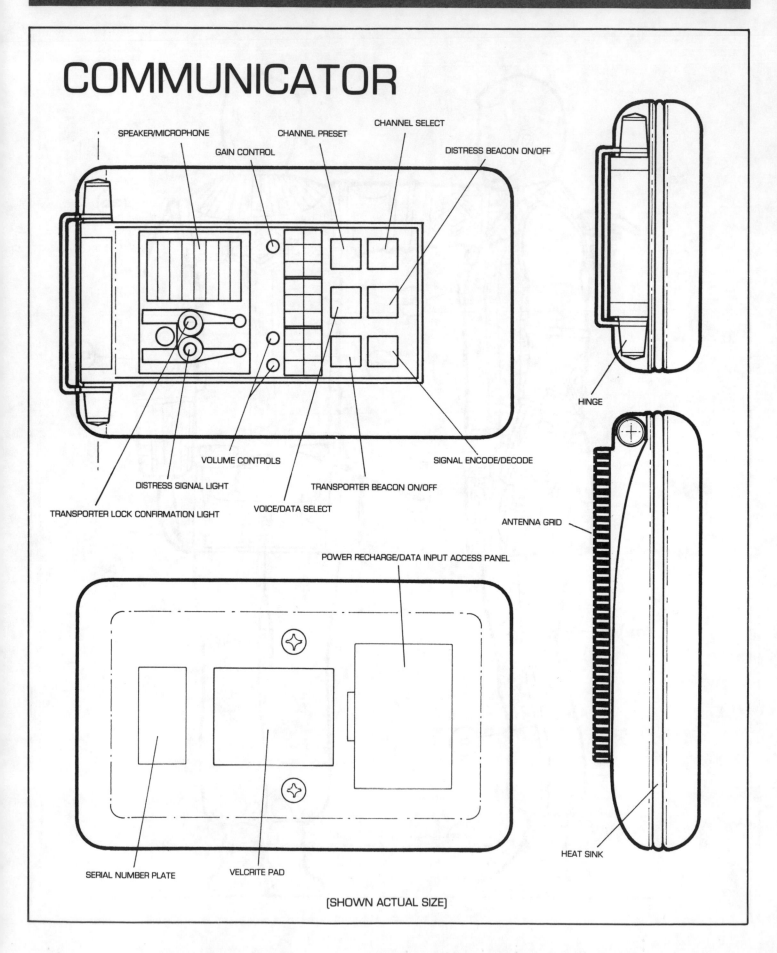

SPEAKER/MICROPHONE

GAIN CONTROL

CHANNEL PRESET

CHANNEL SELECT

DISTRESS BEACON ON/OFF

HINGE

VOLUME CONTROLS

DISTRESS SIGNAL LIGHT

TRANSPORTER LOCK CONFIRMATION LIGHT

VOICE/DATA SELECT

TRANSPORTER BEACON ON/OFF

SIGNAL ENCODE/DECODE

ANTENNA GRID

POWER RECHARGE/DATA INPUT ACCESS PANEL

SERIAL NUMBER PLATE

VELCRITE PAD

HEAT SINK

[SHOWN ACTUAL SIZE]

TRICORDER

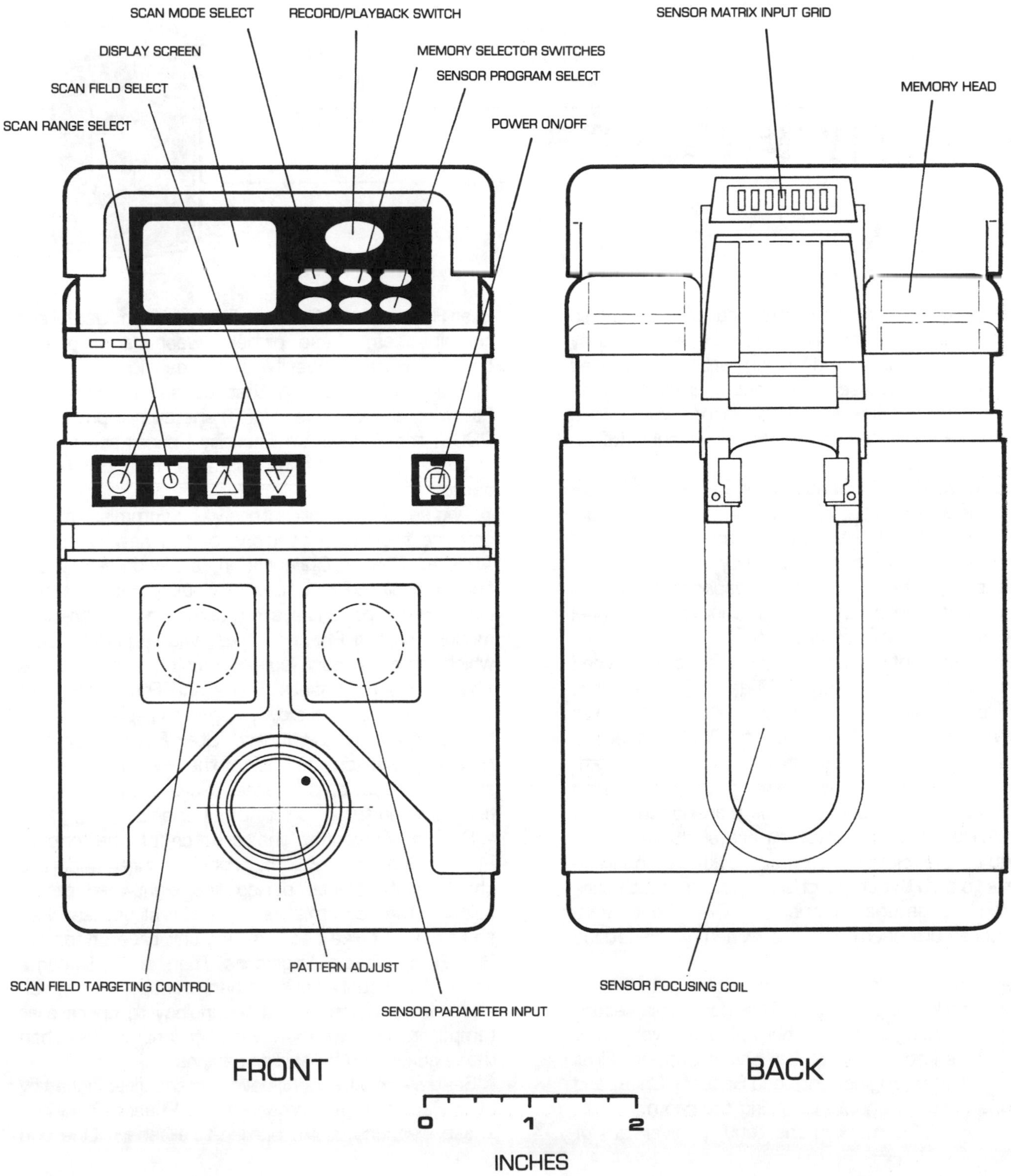

SCAN MODE SELECT

RECORD/PLAYBACK SWITCH

DISPLAY SCREEN

MEMORY SELECTOR SWITCHES

SCAN FIELD SELECT

SENSOR PROGRAM SELECT

SCAN RANGE SELECT

POWER ON/OFF

SENSOR MATRIX INPUT GRID

MEMORY HEAD

SCAN FIELD TARGETING CONTROL

PATTERN ADJUST

SENSOR PARAMETER INPUT

SENSOR FOCUSING COIL

FRONT

BACK

0 1 2

INCHES

minor impacts have evoked a discontinuance of the unit.

Tricorders now used aboard ship are similar in function and appearance to the black flip-top model still in use throughout much of the Federation, with a retrac-

table memory head replacing the microdisc system used on older models. Maximum range for the sciences tricorder is 3900 feet; the medical version can scan objects up to 490 feet away.

ARMORY/PHASERS

Enterprise's main armory is located adjacent to the main briefing room on G Deck. Here, weaponry for security personnel and landing party use is stored within a locked, phaser resistant chamber. All armory bulkheads are lined with diburnium-osmium alloy, the same metal upon which the vessel's deflectors are based.

Access to the weapons storage chamber is furnished via a reinforced door on one wall of the armory foyer. The clearance desk outside the door is manned at all times by two security officers, whose duty it is to check in and out all weaponry. Palmprint identification insures that no unauthorized personnel check out equipment at any time.

A wide range of weapon types and sizes are stored within the armory chamber. Phasers Three, Four, and Five are stored in quantity, as are the newer Phaser One-B and Two-B units. Photon grenade mortars, gas grenades, timed explosives, communications lasers, phaser power packs, restraining cuffs, utility belts, subcutaneous transponders, and portable force field projectors are all stored here. Enough phaser pistols, stored in racks, are contained here to arm the entire crew, if necessary. Security armor hangs against one wall. One phaser cannon, stored disassembled, is provided for planetside use.

The chamber door is unlocked by punching a preset code into a panel beside the door. This security code is changed at the beginning of every duty shift, and is known only to the ship's Captain, First Officer, Chief of Engineering, and Security Chief, and to those security agents guarding the room.

October 2216 marked the tenth anniversary of

Star Fleet's use of Phasers One and Two. Useful and reliable allies, these pioneer weapons of phaser technology made possible the expansion of Federation boundaries during that decade of discovery. Following the discovery of Transtator II physics in 2209, the Federation Security Council determined by majority vote that these basic arms should be updated.

Two separate contractors were commissioned to produce their own versions of the new weapons. Atalskes Phaser Corporation, a newcomer to the field, translated the new technology into a sleek, bluegray component system combining a palm-sized module (named Phaser Three) with a pistol mount which forms a more powerful unit (referred to as Phaser Four). Phasers Three and Four were first issued in 2212, and slowly began to replace Phaser One and Two units aboard Star Fleet vessels. A touchkey panel on the back of the Phaser Three unit allowed the device's internal micro-computer to be programmed for a variety of functions.

Sestra Weapons, the creator of the original Phaser One/Two system, produced three separate phaser instruments during the eight-year period following their commissioning. The first of these was an advanced pulse-beam mining unit created for the Star Fleet Corps of Engineers. Then, in 2215, came a new ship-mounted phaser bank configuration which also utilized Transtator II technology to operate at temperatures twenty-seven percent cooler than those generated by earlier designs.

Sestra's most recent development, first issued by Star Fleet this past year, is the Phaser B series. These weapons, quite similar to Phasers One and

PHASER IV

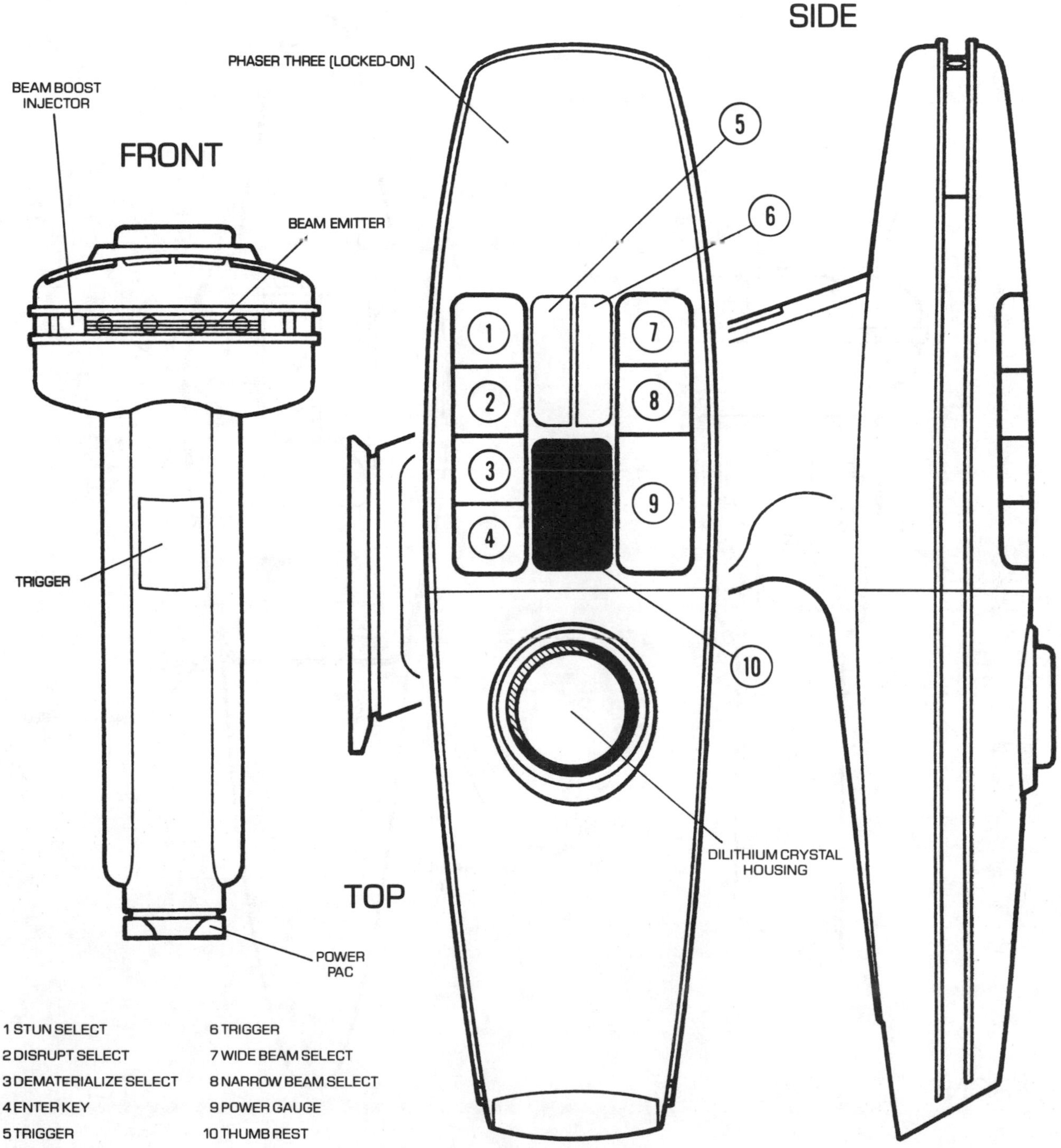

SIDE

PHASER THREE [LOCKED-ON]

BEAM BOOST
INJECTOR

FRONT

BEAM EMITTER

⑤

⑥

① ⑦

② ⑧

③ ⑨

④

⑩

TRIGGER

DILITHIUM CRYSTAL
HOUSING

TOP

POWER
PAC

1 STUN SELECT	6 TRIGGER
2 DISRUPT SELECT	7 WIDE BEAM SELECT
3 DEMATERIALIZE SELECT	8 NARROW BEAM SELECT
4 ENTER KEY	9 POWER GAUGE
5 TRIGGER	10 THUMB REST

[SHOWN ACTUAL SIZE]

PHASER IIB

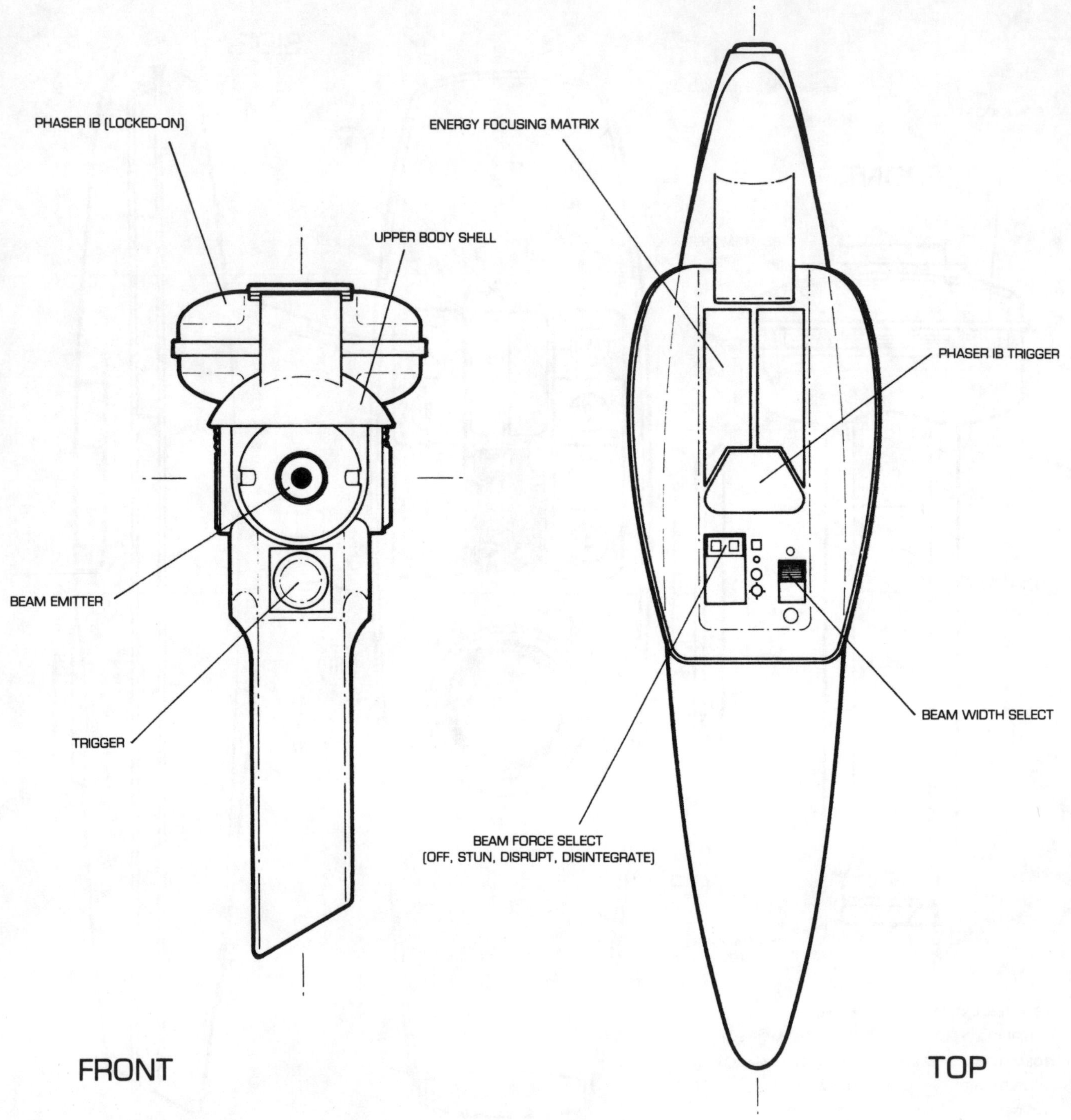

PHASER IB (LOCKED-ON)

ENERGY FOCUSING MATRIX

UPPER BODY SHELL

PHASER IB TRIGGER

BEAM EMITTER

TRIGGER

BEAM WIDTH SELECT

BEAM FORCE SELECT
(OFF, STUN, DISRUPT, DISINTEGRATE)

FRONT

TOP

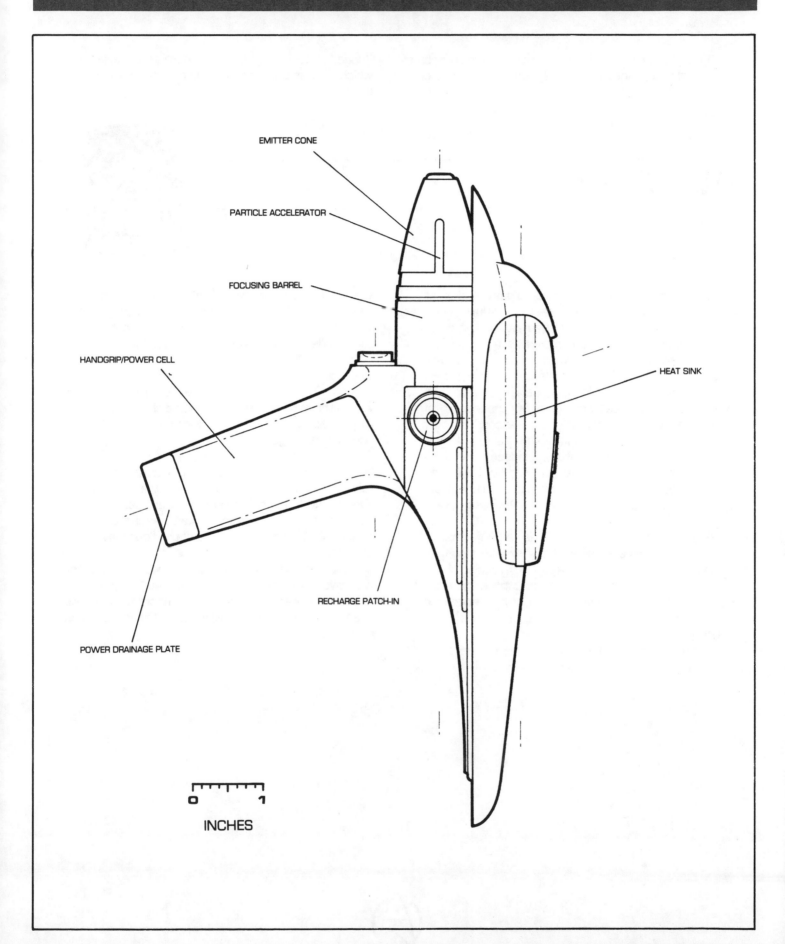

EMITTER CONE

PARTICLE ACCELERATOR

FOCUSING BARREL

HANDGRIP/POWER CELL

HEAT SINK

RECHARGE PATCH-IN

POWER DRAINAGE PLATE

0   1

INCHES

Two, feature a few minor changes which accommodate new internal cooling and control systems. The One-B and Two-B units have a much simpler "speed setting" system of beam force selection, which in tests proved invaluable during personal combat situations.

REC DECK

Enterprise's rec deck is the largest and best equipped of any in Star Fleet. Off-duty crew members will find a variety of games and pastimes from which to choose within its walls.

At the front of the room is an immense, wall-mounted viewing screen, the largest aboard ship. This three-dimensional imaging device can be programmed to display any one of thousands of twentieth-, twenty-first, or twenty-second century movies, and also holds in its memory a lesser number of twenty-third century releases. Live sporting events, carried by subspace video comlink, can be displayed as well. On rare occasion, the unit is used to display Star Fleet Personnel Address broadcasts for crew assemblies.

Beneath the viewing screen is an information display alcove. Five small screens exhibit, upon request, a choice of pictorial histories, including those of Star Fleet, the Federation, the countries on Earth, Vulcan, Alpha Centauri, and other Federation worlds, and all vessels which have borne the name "Enterprise."

Reading lounges and snack bars line the port and starboard bulkheads. Restrooms, designated "male" (portside) and "female" (starboard) for the convenience of non-crew visitors, are located near the rec deck's rear wall on the lower level.

Two turbolifts on the forward end of the room provide access to F Deck and the rec deck's balcony around. This upper area houses smaller rooms where three-dimensional chess and checkers may be played, as well as cards, backgammon, and other non-electronic games.

A raised platform in the center of the lower level floor features a diversity of electronic entertainments. Games such as Concentrex, Challenge, Eye-Q, and Phaser Duel are programmed into consoles which stand within sunken seating areas. A shufflelight board in the middle of the floor may be used for tournament play.

Eight immense viewports in the rec deck's outer wall give crew members an unspoiled view of the ship's secondary hull and warp nacelles, and are useful for planet observation while Enterprise is in standard orbit.

REC DECK (LOWER LEVEL)

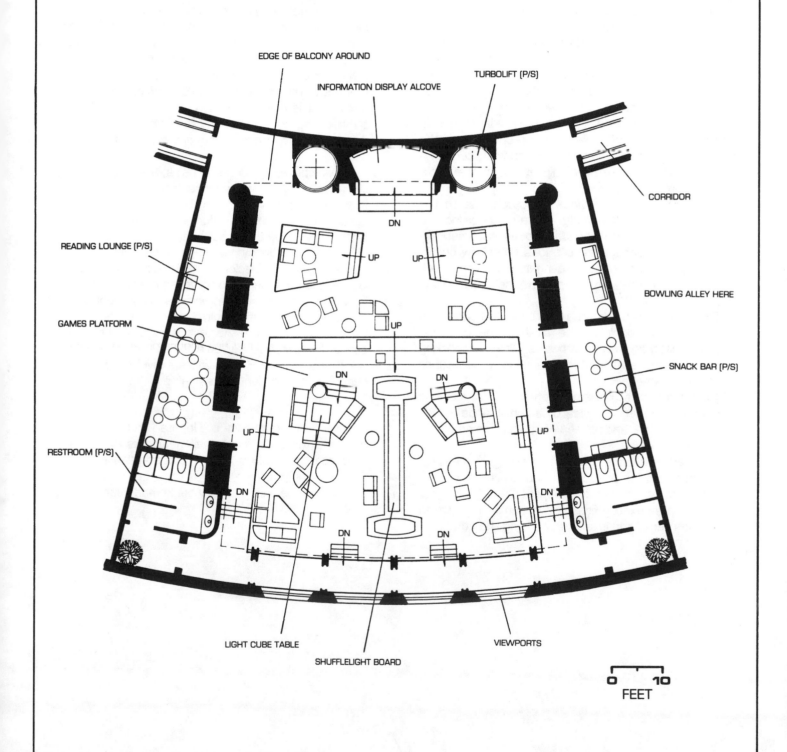

EDGE OF BALCONY AROUND

INFORMATION DISPLAY ALCOVE

TURBOLIFT (P/S)

CORRIDOR

READING LOUNGE (P/S)

BOWLING ALLEY HERE

GAMES PLATFORM

SNACK BAR (P/S)

RESTROOM (P/S)

DN

UP

UP

UP

DN

DN

UP

UP

DN

DN

DN

DN

LIGHT CUBE TABLE

SHUFFLELIGHT BOARD

VIEWPORTS

0   10
FEET

H Deck is often referred to as the "docking level" for it features the primary hull's two main docking port complexes. Each is fully equipped to handle any extravehicular need.

Two huge sliding doors, flush with the outer hull when closed, conceal each docking bay. These doors are composed of reinforced trititanium and are controlled from a console within the complex.

A staging area provides access to both a personnel airlock and a standard docking port. Here, crew members leaving the ship may don spacesuits, when necessary. Four suits are contained in wall-mounted lockers, which also feature recharge systems for the suits' life support and power units.

The personnel airlock runs alongside the main docking airlock, and opens via hatchway into the docking bay. This room allows spacesuited EVA crews to enter and exit the ship while a craft is docked to the main port.

A radial corridor provides direct access to the staging area of each complex. A safety door located at a point along the corridor closes automatically should catastrophic pressure loss somehow occur. A safety circuit prevents the inner and outer airlock hatches from both being opened when no craft is mated to the port.

Docking procedures are monitored and controlled from a small room to one side of the complex. Double-paned reinforced windows allow the docking supervisor to view the staging area and the interior of the personnel airlock.

An equipment storage bay contains EVA gear and hull repair materials. Nearby maintenance shops handle the repair and upkeep of spacesuits and small equipment.

A departure lounge just off of the staging area provides comfort for passengers while shuttlecraft or travel pods make their final approaches.

The ship's auxiliary fire control center is situated at the center of the level, surrounding the computer core. From this location, all shipboard weapons systems can be controlled manually.

At the rear of the deck is the ship's laundry. Here, all soiled crew uniforms are broken down into their base components and reassembled as fresh clothing. Articles to be cleaned may be placed in the appropriate carrier tubes on each deck.

Enterprise's fabrication facility is also found on H Deck. A number of Chiokis-built, computer-controlled material synthesizers manufacture tools, hardware, clothing, small devices, repair parts, and any other objects which can be programmed into the fabricator matrix, using a stock of raw materials much as the ship's food synthesizers do. Similarly, an adjoining reclamation facility reduces discarded items down to their component elements for later use.

Six viewports, arranged in pairs, are located along the level's outer concentric corridor. Also, the primary hull's lower phaser banks are mounted in hardpoints at the bow, port, and starboard positions, behind the outer bulkheads.

Should emergency hull separation ever become necessary, the H Deck level of the connecting dorsal is designed to perform several major functions. Couplings in the vertical intermix shaft disconnect at this level, and explosive bolts beneath the floor sever the primary hull from the rest of the ship. Once the saucer has safely landed on a planet surface, the forward floor of the H Deck dorsal level drops down, becoming an ingress/egress ramp.

Three viewing lounges are located on I Deck. Each of these features four small viewports, which are built into the flooring beyond a protective handrail. The remainder of the level is occupied by the M-6 computer's backup memory banks and supercooling system.

DOCKING PORT COMPLEX

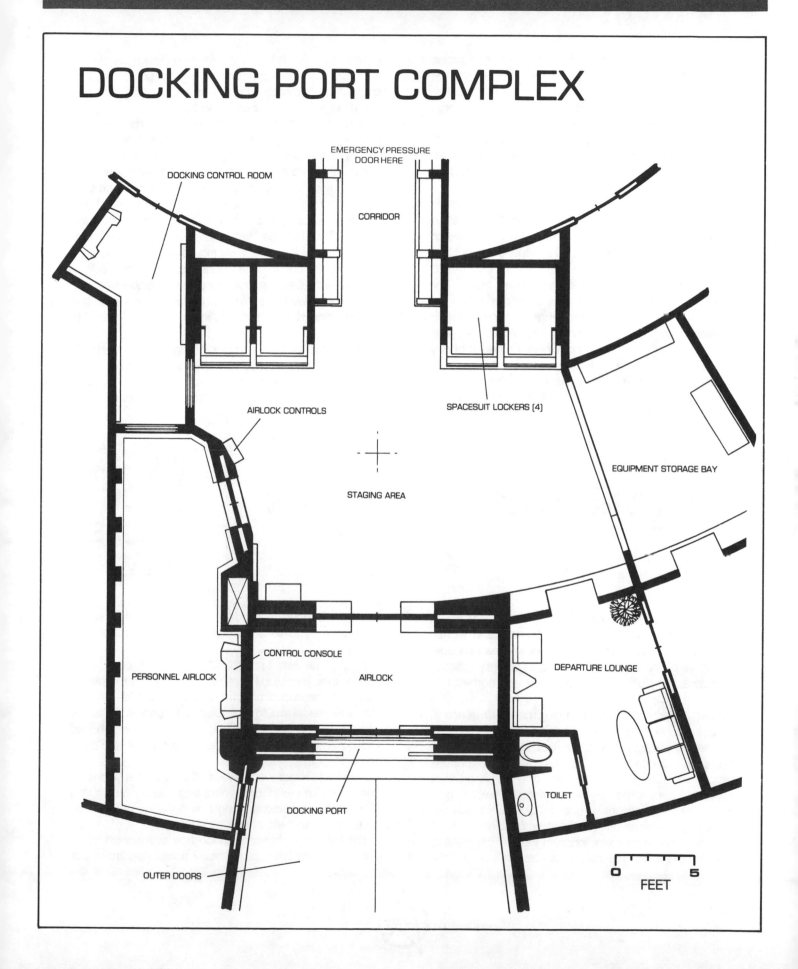

DOCKING CONTROL ROOM

EMERGENCY PRESSURE
DOOR HERE

CORRIDOR

SPACESUIT LOCKERS [4]

AIRLOCK CONTROLS

STAGING AREA

EQUIPMENT STORAGE BAY

CONTROL CONSOLE

DEPARTURE LOUNGE

PERSONNEL AIRLOCK

AIRLOCK

DOCKING PORT

TOILET

OUTER DOORS

0   5
FEET

J Deck consists entirely of the primary hull circuit breaker room. From here, power to all of the saucer's internal systems is monitored both manually and by computer, insuring that unexpected energy surges do no damage to shipboard equipment.

K Deck, also a single room, is the main sensor array monitoring station. Two science specialists man this facility. A stairway up leads to the turbolift door on J Deck, the bottom of the elevator shaft.

Housed within the connecting dorsal, between H and I Decks, is a three-feet thick hull separation system layer. This unit uses magnetic repulsors to widen the initial gap between the separating hulls.

Specialized passenger staterooms are found within the I-K Deck dorsal levels. These cabins are capable of maintaining the environments often required by non-humanoid passengers. Atmospheric variations, including ammonia, hot methane, and seawater, fulfill the life support requirements of any member species of the Federation. These specially insulated compartments require, on the average, four hours of preparation time before occupancy.

A small, transparent aluminum platform, like those found on the warp engineering levels, encircles the intermix shaft on each of the dorsal levels. Accessed by one-man lifts, these monitoring stations are manned by engineering personnel.

A turbolift shaft runs vertically, in semi-stairstep fashion, near the back of the connecting dorsal. Enterprise's newly designed Jeffries tube connects the F Deck impulse engine room with the upper level of warp engineering on N Deck. Vital power and propulsion circuitry is accessed within this angled shaft, which runs along the entire back of the connecting dorsal. The Jeffries tube is diburnium-osmium reinforced for added safety during combat situations.

A vertical ladder tube connects the I Deck dorsal level with N Deck in the warp engineering section. This passageway provides access between the primary and secondary hulls in the event of turbolift failure.

All primary hull-to-dorsal openings [turbolift shafts, ladderways, piping/wiring trunks, and Jeffries tube] seal off automatically at the separation line just prior to emergency disconnection.

PHOTORP LAUNCH SYSTEM

The foundation levels of the connecting dorsal, L and M Decks, contain the photon torpedo launch system. This two-story facility handles the storage, arming and loading of the ship's twenty photon torpedoes (or "photorps," as they are sometimes called).

When originally refitted during her five years in drydock, Enterprise was equipped with a fully automated photorp launch system. All loading and firing procedures were handled at the weapons station on the main bridge; this arrangement shortened firing order-to-launch time by twenty percent over common manual launch systems. However, an unforseen overheating problem plagued the auto-arming system, aborting seven percent of all attempted launchings. This design utilized the Morris Magtronics Model FP-4 torpedo, the same type used by Enterprise during her years as a Constitution class starship.

Enterprise was brought into the newly-completed space dock facility in November of 2220 for replacement of the entire photorp system. It was decided that the vessel would be equipped to handle Beltesha Missile Systems' new Mark VI torpedo, which had tested so successfully at the Arcturus Deep Space Firing Range.

L and M Decks were modified to house a two-level complex of photorp storage and launching machinery. A backup firing computer was installed on L Deck, just aft of the turboshaft.

Enterprise's photorp launch bay is manned at all times, though firing is normally controlled from the bridge. Storage racks for the photorp casings are located on L Deck; a loading arm magnetically clutches each casing to be fired and inserts it into an arming recepticle, where a matter/antimatter charge is injected and primed.

Once the explosive payload is in place, the casing travels aftward by overhead rail then down to the M Deck launch system. There, the loading arm releases the armed photorp, and it is carried into the launch tube by magnetic carrier.

The torpedo launch tube is U-shaped, creating two ejection points from which photorps may be fired. Each side of the tube is capable of holding four armed torpedoes at ready, for rapid-fire situations. The vertical intermix shaft is mounted between the arms of the launch tube, as is the dorsal's emergency ladderway.

At the rear of L Deck, surrounding the Jeffries tube, is the photon exhaust system. Whenever a torpedo is fired, this mechanism forcefully ejects superheated gases aftward through a vent matrix in the outer hull, this countering the inertial forces created by the departing photorp. While these forces are quite small, they can disrupt the kinetic balance of a vessel in motion or even propel a ship as it attempts to keep station.

M Deck also features port and starboard docking ports. The portside hatch opens into an airlock, through which one may enter either the torpedo bay or the turbolift lobby. The starboard port gives access to a small airlock and storage room. An observation lounge is contained on the port side, just forward of the main airlock.

The rear portion of M Deck houses the photorp auxiliary fire control room and toilet facilities.

Portside airlock entry into Photorp launch bay

PHOTON TORPEDO ROOM

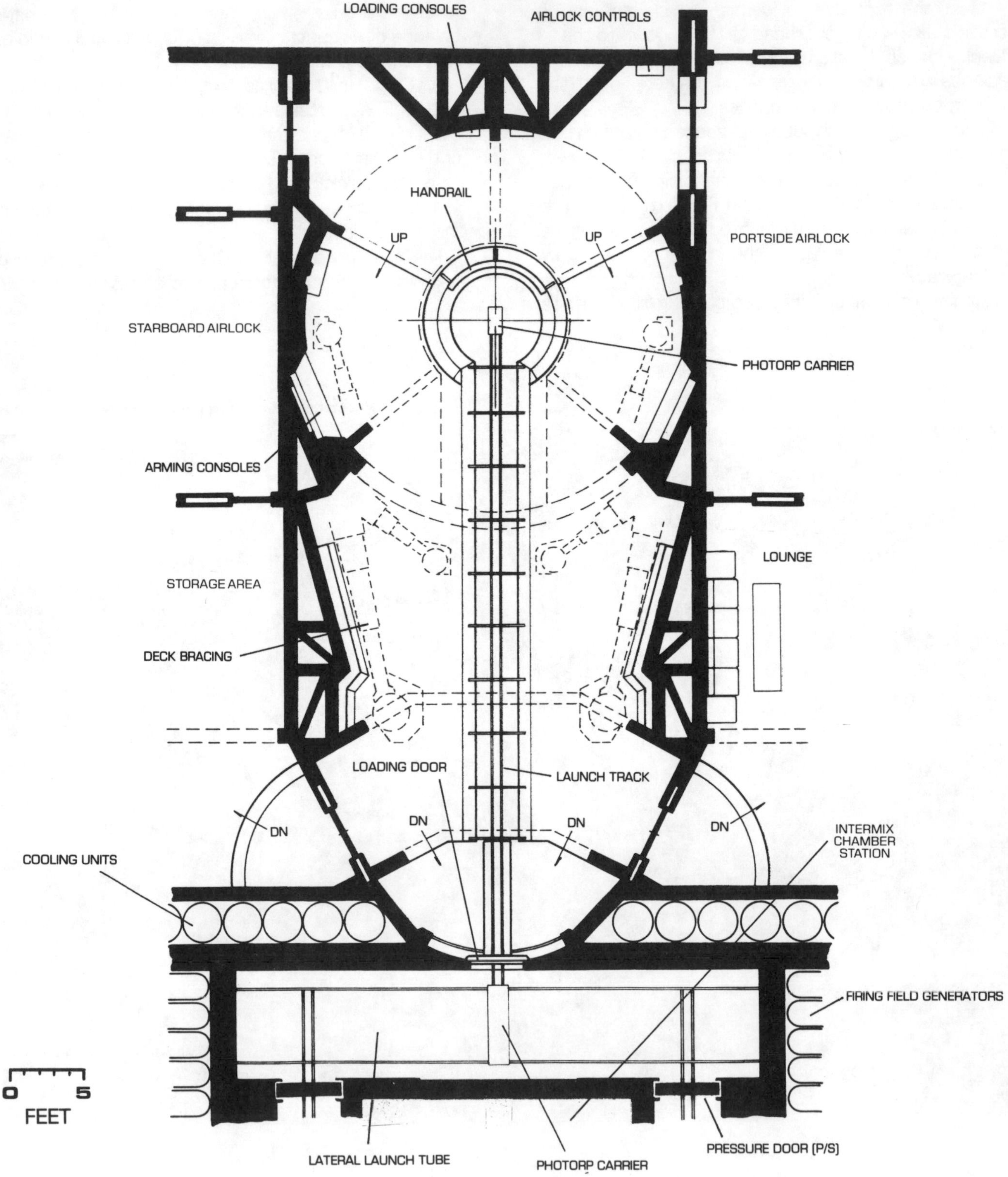

LOADING CONSOLES

AIRLOCK CONTROLS

HANDRAIL

UP

UP

PORTSIDE AIRLOCK

STARBOARD AIRLOCK

PHOTORP CARRIER

ARMING CONSOLES

LOUNGE

STORAGE AREA

DECK BRACING

LOADING DOOR

LAUNCH TRACK

DN

DN

DN

DN

INTERMIX
CHAMBER
STATION

COOLING UNITS

FIRING FIELD GENERATORS

0   5
FEET

LATERAL LAUNCH TUBE

PHOTORP CARRIER

PRESSURE DOOR [P/S]

PHOTORP [MARK VI]

SIDE

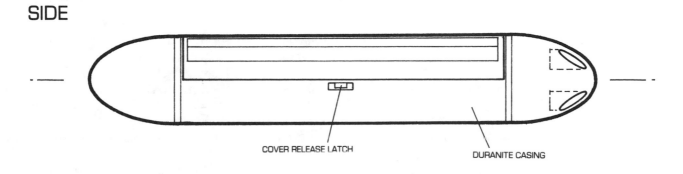

COVER RELEASE LATCH   DURANITE CASING

PAYLOAD BAY COVER

TOP

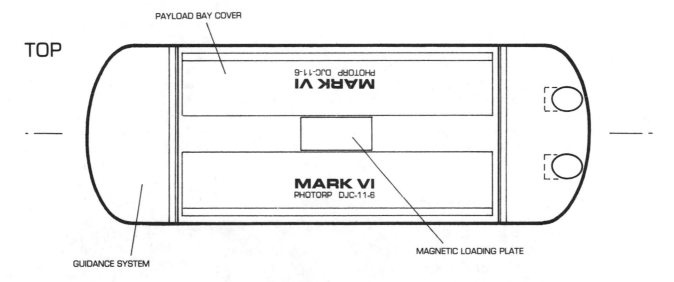

MARK VI
PHOTORP DJC-11-6

MARK VI
PHOTORP DJC-11-6

GUIDANCE SYSTEM

MAGNETIC LOADING PLATE

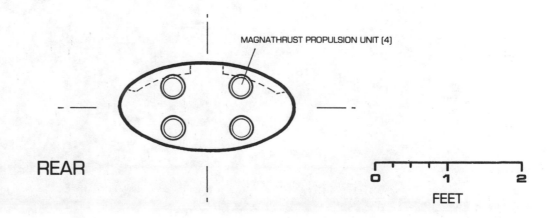

MAGNATHRUST PROPULSION UNIT [4]

REAR

0   1   2

FEET

WARP ENGINEERING

Enterprise's warp engineering section is lodged on N and O Decks. All thrust and power systems are primarily controlled from this site, as is the ship's life support and gravity control equipment.

N Deck is the uppermost level of the secondary hull. It serves as the structural support strongback of the ship, and is the anchoring framework for the connecting dorsal and the warp nacelle pylons. On the forward end of the level is the engineering computer monitoring room, which encircles the vertical intermix shaft and opens, to the rear, into the engineering computer bay. The rear bulkhead of the computer bay contains an emergency section door which lowers to O Deck and separates the warp engine room from the extended horizontal intermix area; the door drops automatically in the event of a radiation leak or pressure loss.

A narrow corridor bypasses the computer bay on the port side and leads aftward down the center of the level. On either side of this passageway are mounted the four maneuvering thrusters which rest beneath the upper hull of the secondary hull strongback. These thrusters are used for vessel course control when within close proximity of drydock facilities. A turbolift accesses the starboard side of the corridor.

At the aft end of N Deck is the bottom of the Jeffries tube.

Ceiling height in the monitoring room and the computer bay is twelve feet [the standard height for each level of the secondary hull]; the remainder of N Deck has a higher floor level and a ceiling height of nine feet.

O Deck is often referred to simply as "engineering." Enterprise's warp engine room, forward on this level, is the result of more than nine years of intensive research and development. Every aspect of its layout contributes to a faster crew member reaction time, with each control panel duplicated in some manner on the main bridge for improved command

Warp engineering section w/vertical intermix chamber

WARP ENGINE ROOM

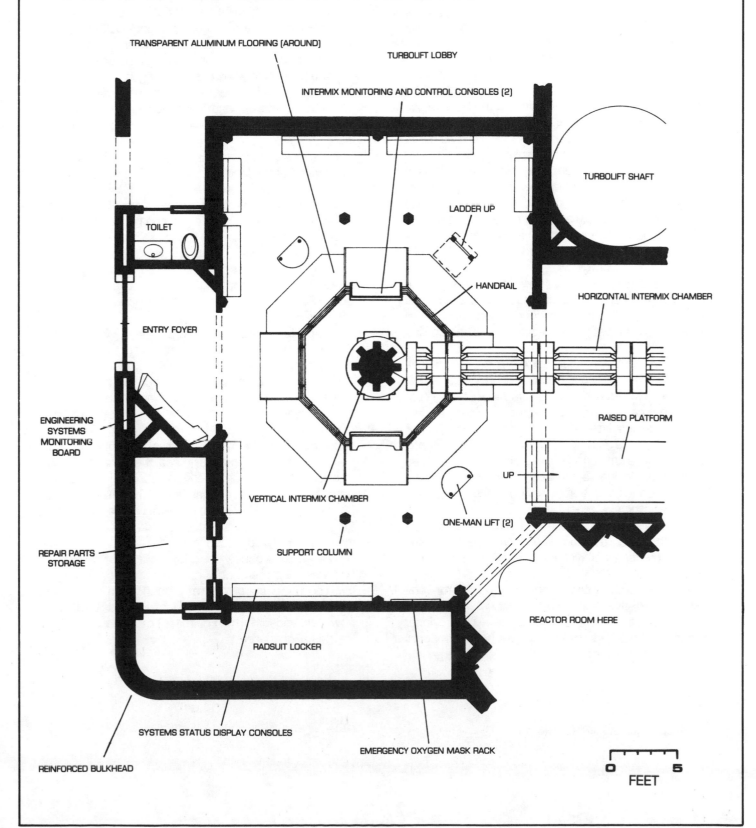

TRANSPARENT ALUMINUM FLOORING [AROUND]

TURBOLIFT LOBBY

INTERMIX MONITORING AND CONTROL CONSOLES [2]

TURBOLIFT SHAFT

TOILET

LADDER UP

HANDRAIL

HORIZONTAL INTERMIX CHAMBER

ENTRY FOYER

ENGINEERING
SYSTEMS
MONITORING
BOARD

RAISED PLATFORM

UP

VERTICAL INTERMIX CHAMBER

ONE-MAN LIFT [2]

REPAIR PARTS
STORAGE

SUPPORT COLUMN

REACTOR ROOM HERE

RADSUIT LOCKER

SYSTEMS STATUS DISPLAY CONSOLES

EMERGENCY OXYGEN MASK RACK

REINFORCED BULKHEAD

0   FEET   5

monitoring and interaction capability.

Located in the center of the room, and extending for many levels both above and below the deck, is the vertical linear intermix chamber. This complex, radically new design in intermix technology provides operational power for the impulse drive system and furnishes enough additional energy to power all other shipboard systems. Both matter and antimatter for the chamber are contained in a series of magnetic bottles, which are housed in pods at the base of the intermix shaft. These pods may be ejected from the ship in case of extreme emergency via two large blow-away panels in the outer hull.

Extending aftward from the vertical shaft is a horizontal chamber which draws its matter/antimatter fuel from the same source. This shaft provides source energy for the warp field nacelles and phaser banks. The linear configuration has proven to be consistently cooler, cleaner, and more efficient than any other system in use today.

The engine room's entry foyer features the main power systems display board and switching console. From here, engineering personnel can monitor all shipboard power usages and override other control boards.

A door in the forward portside bulkhead accesses a room in which repair circuitry and replacement parts are stored. Another door within that room leads into a radsuit storage locker.

Two one-man lifts provide easy access to the various deck levels around the intermix shaft. Transparent aluminum flooring encircles the open power core, as does a protective handrail. Port and starboard control consoles provide a direct interface with all reactor systems.

Various display consoles stand around the room's perimeter. The dilithium reactor room stands beyond a transparent wall in the chamber's aft portside corner.

The horizontal intermix shaft extends for one hundred forty-five feet aftward, at which point it branches out and upward toward the nacelle pylons. Beyond are load-bearing structures (which support the immense mass of the nacelles and pylons) and a narrow corridor which leads to the aft end of the deck.

At the end of this corridor, a double sliding door opens into the landing bay control room. This area features five large windows which look out into space beyond the stern of the ship. The vessel's landing bay doors are controlled from this point, as are the landing tractor beams and the landing bay force field. Three additional viewports afford an upward view of the ship's nacelles, and a floor-level row of windows gives an unobstructed view of the entire landing bay floor.

Enterprise's aft phaser banks are housed on either side of the landing bay control room, above the bay doors atop the aft hull.

A recent addition to Enterprise's warp engineering section is the dilithium reactor room. This radiation-proof chamber was installed while the ship was in drydock for replacement of her photon torpedo system; it provides unobstructed access to the vessel's dilithium couplings, allowing the crystals to be easily replaced in the event of crystal burnout or other damage.

The dilithium couplings are contained in a pedestal in the center of the room. A transparent double wall, which contains radiation-dampening gases between the two panes, insulates the chamber from the remainder of the engine room. A rotating door, also transparent, provides airlock-like access to the reactor room interior.

Overload of the dilithium crystal couplings may cause a leakage of excessive radiation into the room interior. Should this happen, an automatic radiation-dampening system activates which, after several hours, returns the room to a habitable condition. Only major vessel damage, centered in the engineering section, could cause such catastrophic crystal failure as to produce radiation spillage of fatal proportions. Replacement of crystals or repositioning of the mounting couplings may be done manually by removing the dome of the containment pedestal; however, radsuits (with helmets) must be worn during this procedure.

Horizontal intermix chamber (looking aft)

Dilithium reactor room

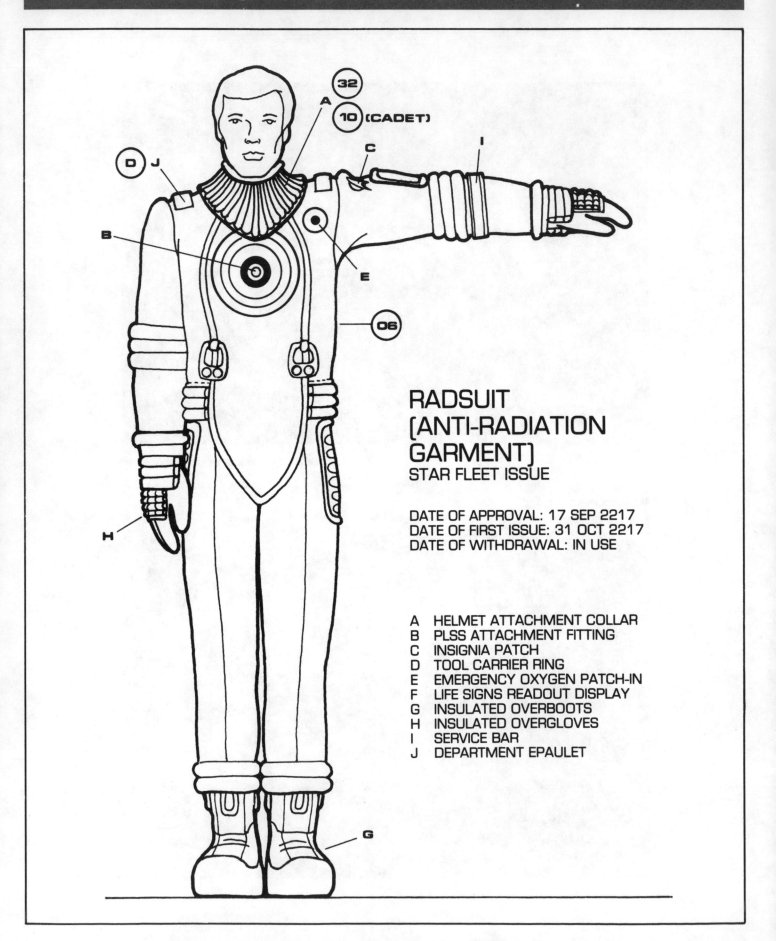

**RADSUIT
(ANTI-RADIATION
GARMENT)**
STAR FLEET ISSUE

DATE OF APPROVAL: 17 SEP 2217
DATE OF FIRST ISSUE: 31 OCT 2217
DATE OF WITHDRAWAL: IN USE

A   HELMET ATTACHMENT COLLAR
B   PLSS ATTACHMENT FITTING
C   INSIGNIA PATCH
D   TOOL CARRIER RING
E   EMERGENCY OXYGEN PATCH-IN
F   LIFE SIGNS READOUT DISPLAY
G   INSULATED OVERBOOTS
H   INSULATED OVERGLOVES
I   SERVICE BAR
J   DEPARTMENT EPAULET

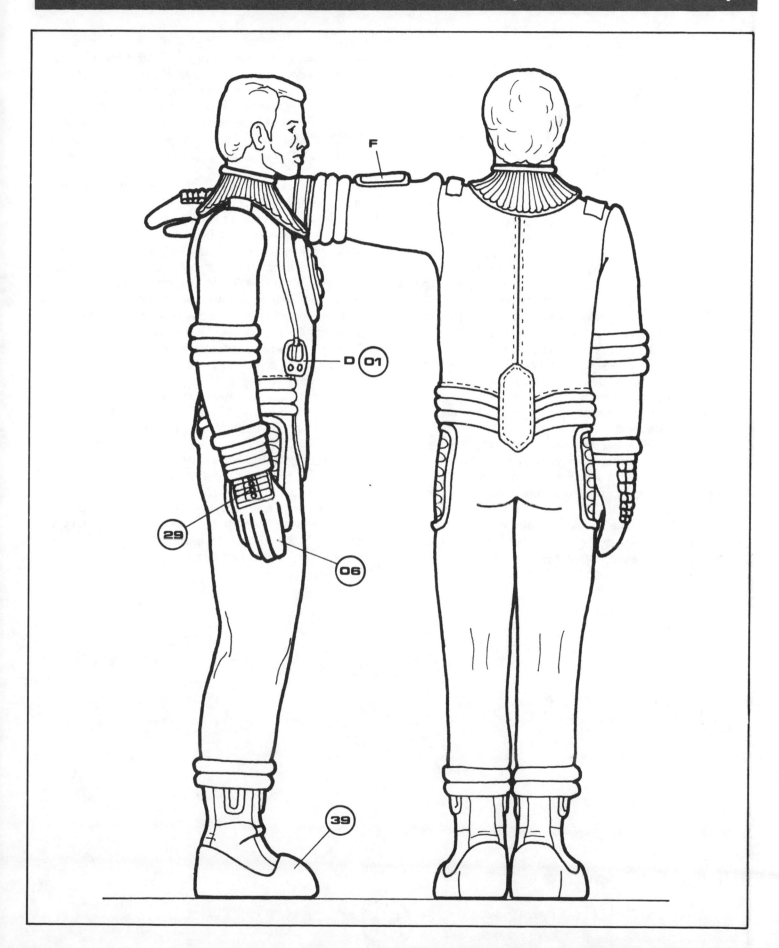

P Deck is primarily an engineering support level. All warp and power subsystems may be found here.

At the forward end of the deck, on either side of the vertical intermix shaft, are twin energy converter units. These large, rounded devices translate the shaft's raw matter/antimatter power into a form which is usable by the vessel's shipboard systems, thus providing electricity and field energy for daily use.

The secondary hull's main stairwell begins on this level, and continues downward for another three decks. This emergency accessway is reinforced, and is fire- and radiation-proof. Pressure-tight doors open onto each deck level, and an indicator within the stairwell, adjacent to each level door, displays the atmospheric status of the deck beyond.

Adjoining the stairway is the secondary hull's main battery room. Twelve nuclear generator cells within this compartment provide backup power should the intermix primary fail. These units cannot furnish enough raw energy to activate the warp nacelles, but do allow the operation of the secondary hull's deflector shield system and all inboard machinery and life support units.

The Chief Engineer's briefing room and office are located on this deck, allowing him easy access to all aspects of the ship's engineering network. Also, in the same area, is the Assistant Chief Engineer's office.

Just aft of the briefing room is Enterprise's primary maintenance complex. This advanced work facility features an unmatched range of tools and equipment, and a variety of specialized shop areas meet the needs of any conceivable repair situation. Specifically-programmed fabricator units within the complex are capable of reproducing any replacement part that might be needed aboard ship. Also housed within this facility is a turbolift repair shop, which is capable of servicing up to four elevator cars at any one time.

At the aft end of P Deck is the open high-bay of the ship's landing bay. On each side, against the outer hull, is an observation gallery which features large, panoramic windows that overlook the floor below.

At the forward end of Q Deck is the secondary hull's emergency transporter facility. Here, two twenty-two man platforms, one on either side of the central intermix room, provide engineering and support personnel with a means of quickly evacuating the secondary hull should such a need arise. Persons may be beamed into the emergency transporters on G Deck, or to a secondary target (such as a planet surface or nearby vessel).

Adjacent to the main stairwell is the circuit breaker room for L-U Decks. This compartment is similar in configuration to that on J Deck.

Q Deck is the main access level of the secondary hull. The aft landing bay provides personnel in small craft with a means of entering or exiting the ship, as do docking ports on either side of the level.

A large open area in the center of the deck serves as the upper inspection balcony of the ship's cargo storage facility. Small observation lounges rim the outer hull on either side of each docking port.

LANDING BAY

Enterprise's new landing bay design incorporates many new developments in Federation technology. A wide range of Star Fleet and Federation craft can utilize this state-of-the-art landing facility in ways never before possible.

Alcoves on either side of the landing bay provide storage for up to six standard workbees, and furnish all necessary recharging and refueling equipment. Additional space is available for the stowage of non-Enterprise shuttlecraft.

Just within the landing bay doors is a force field generator unit, which is built into the main bulkheads on either side of the entry area. This field allows craft to enter the ship, while at the same time retaining the atmosphere and temperature within the landing bay. No vessel may depart, of course, while this one-way barrier is activated.

An auto-landing system is built into the center of the bay floor. This insures that all approaching craft easily clear the opening into the bay.

Flush cargo doors, on either side of the auto-landing track, open to reveal storage holds beneath on R Deck.

An additional feature of the landing bay floor is its variable gravity capability. Different sections may be programmed independently to exert from zero to two-times earth gravity, facilitating a wide range of shuttle maintenance and final checkout procedures.

A landing tractor beam projector is mounted against the P Deck bulkhead, between the observation galleries. This unit is operated from within the landing bay control room.

Two rectangular elevators at the forward end of the landing bay access the two levels beneath Q

View from portside entry port—note shuttlecraft in hangar

Deck, allowing shuttlecraft to travel down to the main hangar and repair facilities.

Small personnel airlocks on either side of the landing bay doors provide admittance to the ship's fantail structure. Each of the two airlocks contains one spacesuit and thruster pack, along with tether lines and other minor EVA equipment.

SHUTTLES/PODS/WORKBEES

Star Fleet's standard personnel shuttlecraft first came into use in September of 2214. Designed and built by Chiokis Starship Construction Corporation, this new vessel differs greatly from the popular Mark 12B model used for so many years.

Chiokis' shuttlecraft configuration incorporates all of the latest available Federation technology. The ship's pilot and co-pilot operate the craft by total instrument guidance; no forward windows are necessary, allowing the installation of a reinforced re-entry shield for atmospheric use. Built into the aft end of the shuttle is a standard docking ring, permitting the ship to hard dock at any vessel or land-based docking port. This capability frees up the landing bays of most vessels for larger craft and cargo ship usage, while permitting personnel to reach their shipboard destinations faster.

The most dramatic change comes in the area of propulsion. Where the Mark 12B shuttle was designed to use ion propulsion (with port and starboard boosters for planetary liftoffs), this new craft utilizes an advanced magnetic field drive. There are no actual thrust ports; all propulsive energies are generated and directed from the two packages on the shuttle's rear sides. This design allows the craft to hover for indefinite periods of time, eliminating the need for wheels or other landing gear and making it possible for the ship to remain stationary just above extremely rough or rocky terrain.

Two mini-phaser banks are mounted to the top of the vessel, and one is recessed into the underside. Also included are protective and navigational deflectors which are stronger than those used on earlier shuttlecraft.

A planetfall hatch on the starboard side of the craft allows ingress and egress when a docking port facility is not available, as when on a planetary surface or for EVAs. A small airlock within permits personnel to open the outer hatch in the presence of toxic or zero atmosphere, without endangering those in the passenger or control compartments.

The ship features seating for six passengers within the rear compartment. A narrow foyer separates this area from the control cabin forward, and also contains two spacesuits and six survival suits.

Four shuttle craft are carried aboard Enterprise. These are numbered One, Three, Five, and Seven, and are named for famous astronomers of the past: Halley [1], Herschel [3], Copernicus [5], and Galileo [7].

The Federation travel pod was originally designed to serve as a small transport and utility vehicle, but has since come to be used almost exclusively as an engineer's inspection car; its large front viewport provides an unmatched view of starship and drydock exteriors as no other small craft can.

The travel pod is designed to provide comfortable transportation for up to six persons. Its interior is capable of full gravity, owing to the development of the miniaturized grav-plate, and optional seating can be installed in minutes, when required.

The pod, like the standard shuttlecraft, is equipped with a standard docking ring for personnel transfer use. Enterprise carries two travel pods within her hangar storage area, where recharging facilities for the pods' particle-beam engines are available.

First used in 2214, the workbee has since become the workhorse of the Federation. Designed as part of a modular construction/support system, the workbee contains the lone crew member needed

SHUTTLECRAFT [STANDARD]

SIDE

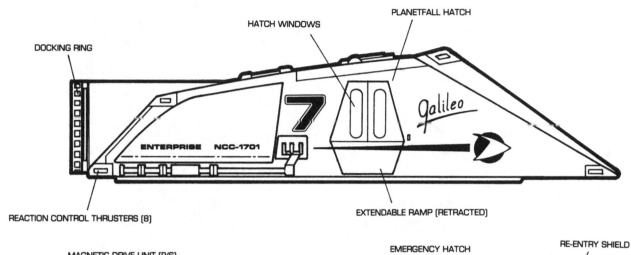

DOCKING RING

HATCH WINDOWS

PLANETFALL HATCH

7

ENTERPRISE NCC-1701

Galileo

REACTION CONTROL THRUSTERS (8)

EXTENDABLE RAMP (RETRACTED)

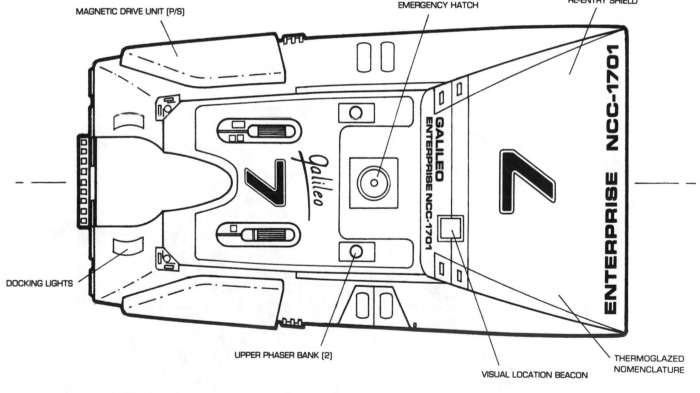

MAGNETIC DRIVE UNIT (P/S)

EMERGENCY HATCH

RE-ENTRY SHIELD

GALILEO ENTERPRISE NCC-1701

GALILEO ENTERPRISE NCC-1701

ENTERPRISE NCC-1701

7

7

Galileo

DOCKING LIGHTS

UPPER PHASER BANK (2)

VISUAL LOCATION BEACON

THERMOGLAZED NOMENCLATURE

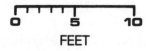

0   5   10

FEET

TOP

TRAVEL POD

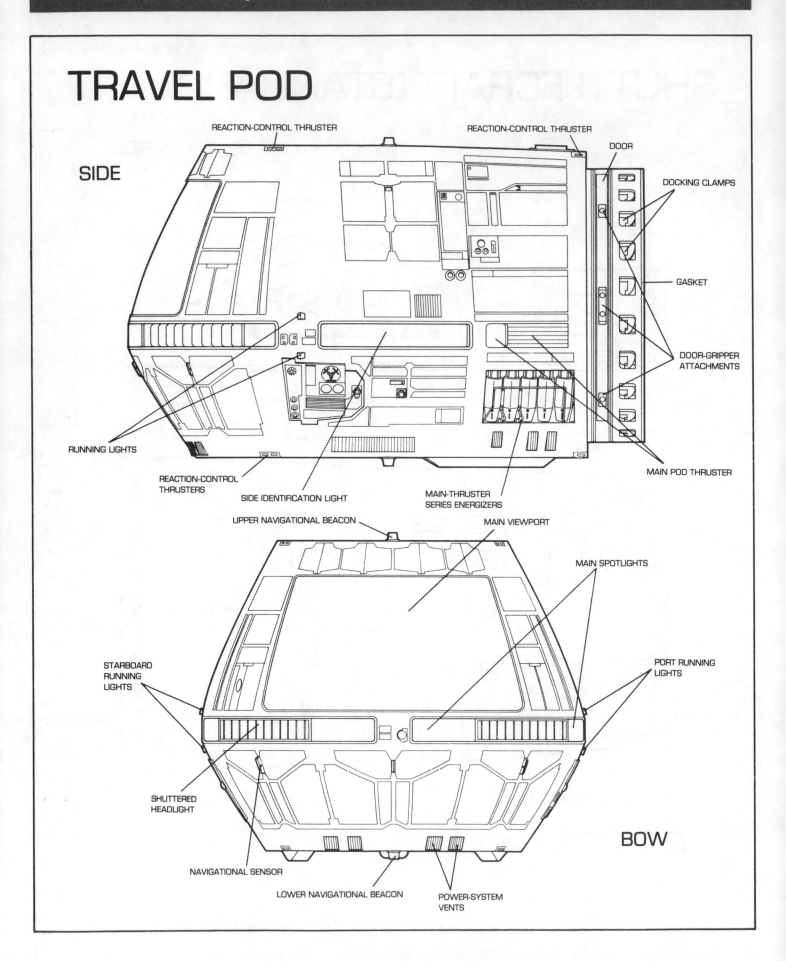

SIDE

REACTION-CONTROL THRUSTER

REACTION-CONTROL THRUSTER

DOOR

DOCKING CLAMPS

GASKET

DOOR-GRIPPER ATTACHMENTS

RUNNING LIGHTS

REACTION-CONTROL THRUSTERS

SIDE IDENTIFICATION LIGHT

MAIN-THRUSTER SERIES ENERGIZERS

MAIN POD THRUSTER

UPPER NAVIGATIONAL BEACON

MAIN VIEWPORT

MAIN SPOTLIGHTS

STARBOARD RUNNING LIGHTS

PORT RUNNING LIGHTS

SHUTTERED HEADLIGHT

NAVIGATIONAL SENSOR

LOWER NAVIGATIONAL BEACON

POWER-SYSTEM VENTS

BOW

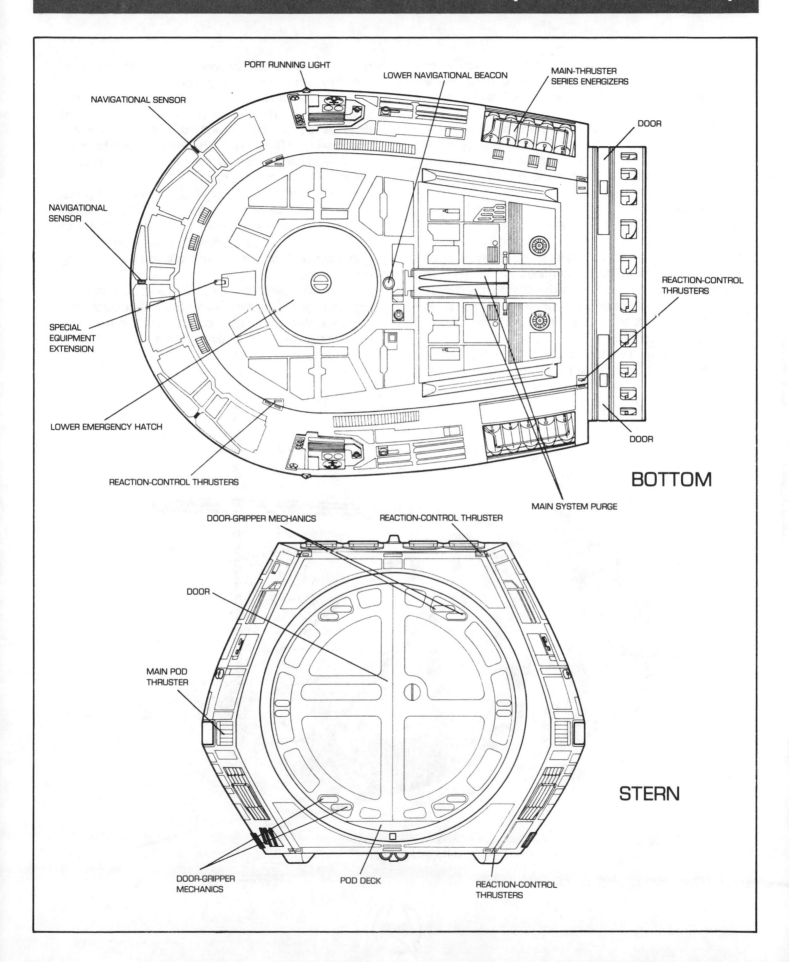

PORT RUNNING LIGHT

LOWER NAVIGATIONAL BEACON

MAIN-THRUSTER SERIES ENERGIZERS

NAVIGATIONAL SENSOR

DOOR

NAVIGATIONAL SENSOR

REACTION-CONTROL THRUSTERS

SPECIAL EQUIPMENT EXTENSION

LOWER EMERGENCY HATCH

DOOR

REACTION-CONTROL THRUSTERS

MAIN SYSTEM PURGE

BOTTOM

DOOR-GRIPPER MECHANICS

REACTION-CONTROL THRUSTER

DOOR

MAIN POD THRUSTER

STERN

DOOR-GRIPPER MECHANICS

POD DECK

REACTION-CONTROL THRUSTERS

for the operation of each unit. Basically an operator's cab, the "bee" can be plugged into a wide variety of specialized work-sleds and towing attachments.

The craft provides full life support for its operator for a period of twelve hours. Artificial gravity is not included, but this is the preference of the vast majority of workbee users as it quickly facilitates EVAs during construction projects.

The bee is often used unpressurized, without its hatch, by spacesuited personnel. During such occasions, life support for the suit can be provided by tanks in the craft, via a retractable umbilical which can extend far beyond the confines of the workbee for EVA usage. Connectors within the craft's cockpit supply power for cutting and welding equipment, as well as for most other powered tools used by construction personnel.

Particle-beam reaction control thrusters furnish primary thrust energy for the workbee. Small sup-

plementary thrusters provide additional forward propulsion when needed, using chemical fuel.

Attachments for the unit include a grabber sled, which utilizes mechanical claws for deep-space damage repair and standard external starship maintenance. The workbee is also designed to pull a specialized cargo train, which can carry up to eight cargo pods at any one time.

The workbee cab soft-docks at any one of six ports within the Enterprise landing bay. These ports feature pressurized walkways that lead directly to the open cab cockpit, allowing crew members in "shirtsleeves" to enter the craft while the landing bay is depressurized.

One recent use of the bee cab is as a control cabin for drydock crane machinery. Special control consoles installed within the cockpit allow the operator to handle a variety of loading arms and construction derricks.

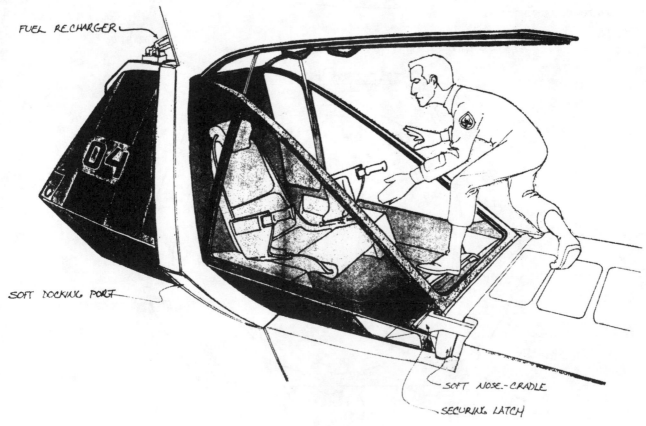

FUEL RECHARGER

04

SOFT DOCKING PORT

SOFT NOSE-CRADLE

SECURING LATCH

CONTRACTORS' SKETCHES

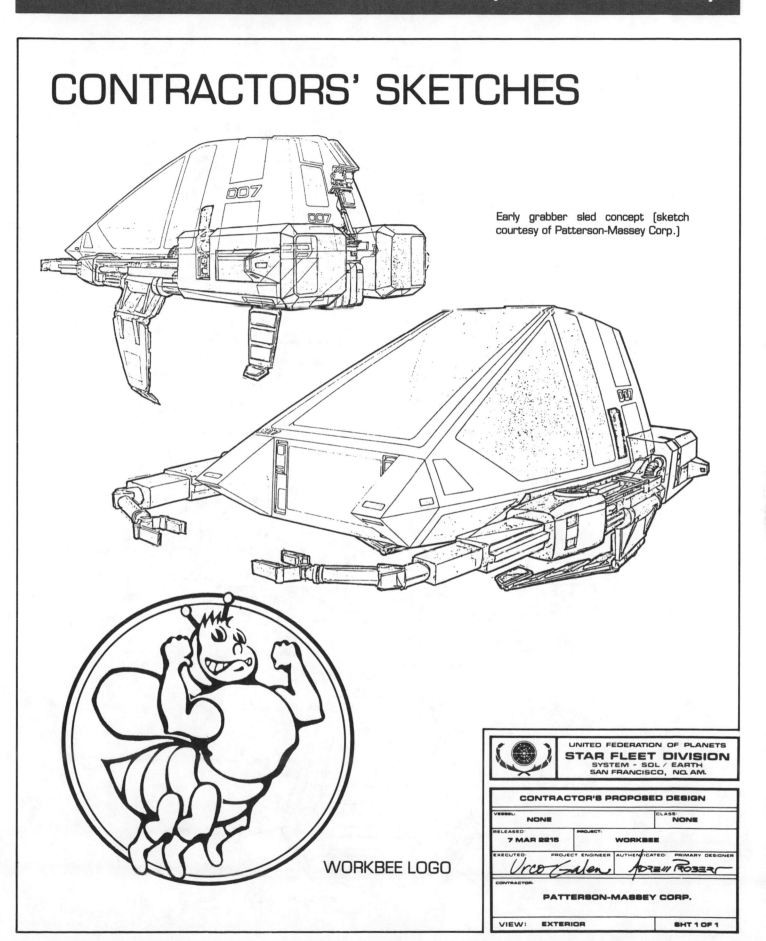

Early grabber sled concept [sketch courtesy of Patterson-Massey Corp.]

WORKBEE LOGO

UNITED FEDERATION OF PLANETS
STAR FLEET DIVISION
SYSTEM - SOL / EARTH
SAN FRANCISCO, NO. AM.

CONTRACTOR'S PROPOSED DESIGN

VESSEL: NONE		CLASS: NONE
RELEASED: **7 MAR 2215**	PROJECT: **WORKBEE**	
EXECUTED: PROJECT ENGINEER	AUTHENTICATED: PRIMARY DESIGNER	
CONTRACTOR:		
PATTERSON-MASSEY CORP.		
VIEW: **EXTERIOR**		**SHT 1 OF 1**

WORKBEE

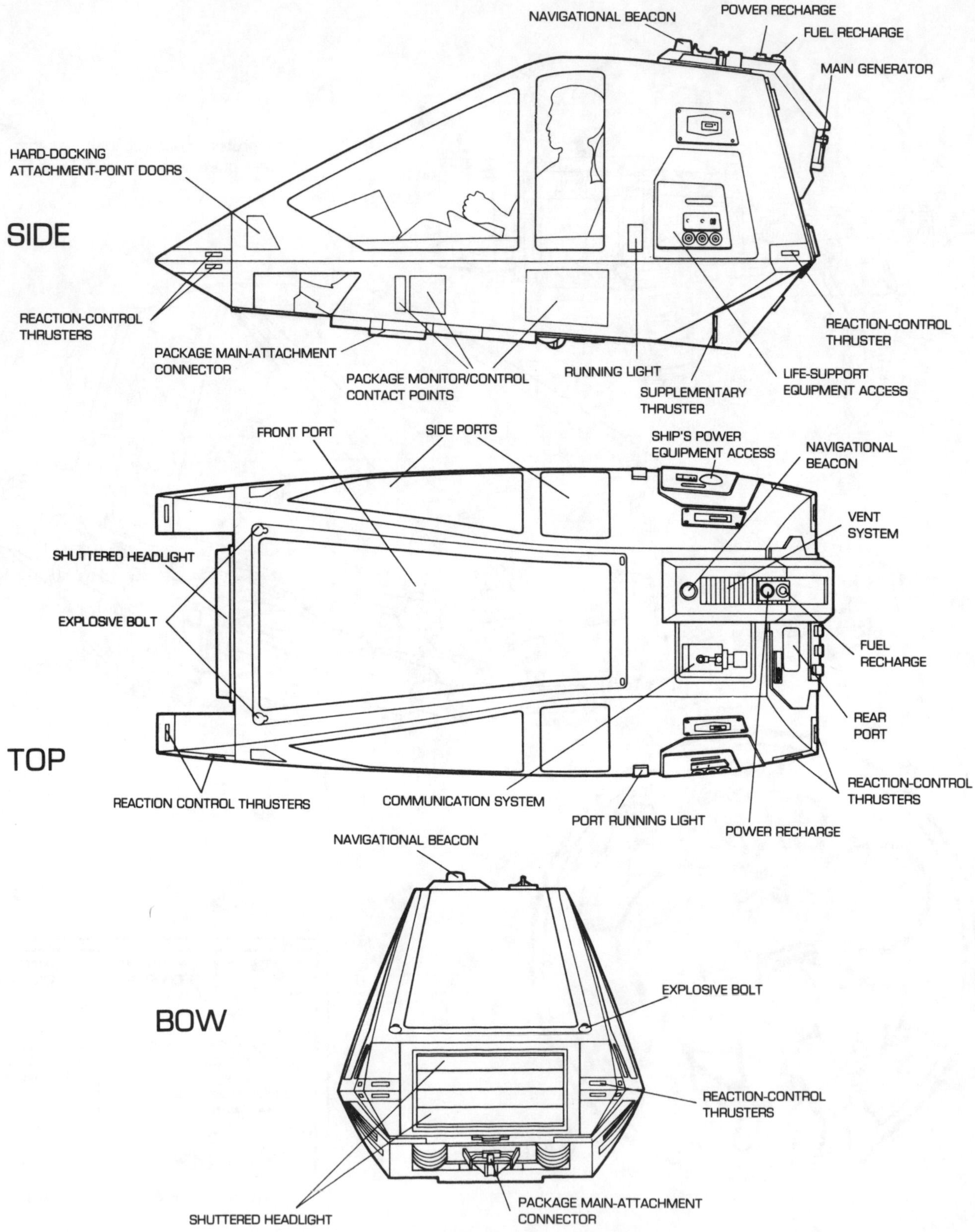

SIDE

NAVIGATIONAL BEACON
POWER RECHARGE
FUEL RECHARGE
MAIN GENERATOR

HARD-DOCKING
ATTACHMENT-POINT DOORS

REACTION-CONTROL
THRUSTERS

PACKAGE MAIN-ATTACHMENT
CONNECTOR

PACKAGE MONITOR/CONTROL
CONTACT POINTS

RUNNING LIGHT

SUPPLEMENTARY
THRUSTER

REACTION-CONTROL
THRUSTER

LIFE-SUPPORT
EQUIPMENT ACCESS

TOP

FRONT PORT

SIDE PORTS

SHIP'S POWER
EQUIPMENT ACCESS

NAVIGATIONAL
BEACON

VENT
SYSTEM

SHUTTERED HEADLIGHT

EXPLOSIVE BOLT

FUEL
RECHARGE

REAR
PORT

REACTION-CONTROL
THRUSTERS

REACTION CONTROL THRUSTERS

COMMUNICATION SYSTEM

PORT RUNNING LIGHT

POWER RECHARGE

BOW

NAVIGATIONAL BEACON

EXPLOSIVE BOLT

REACTION-CONTROL
THRUSTERS

SHUTTERED HEADLIGHT

PACKAGE MAIN-ATTACHMENT
CONNECTOR

GRABBER SLED ATTACHMENT

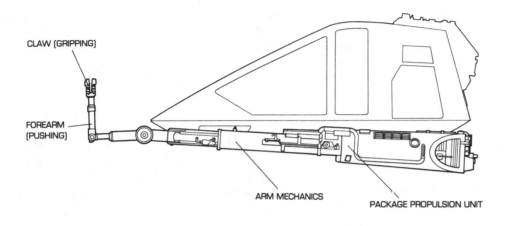

CLAW [GRIPPING]

FOREARM
[PUSHING]

ARM MECHANICS

PACKAGE PROPULSION UNIT

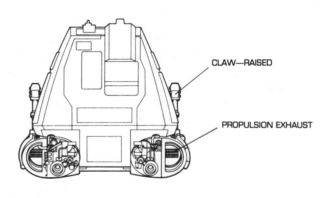

CLAW—RAISED

PROPULSION EXHAUST

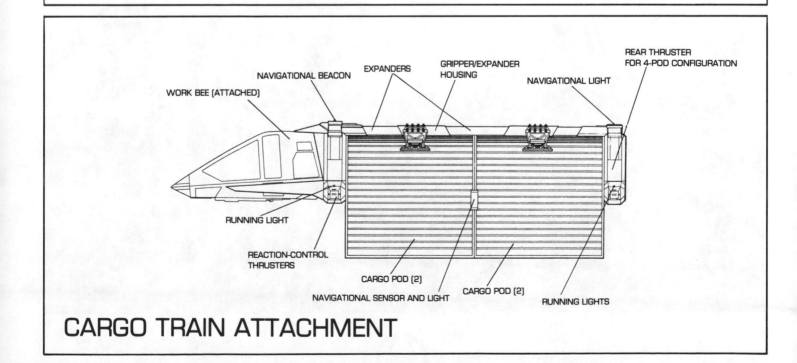

WORK BEE [ATTACHED]

NAVIGATIONAL BEACON

EXPANDERS

GRIPPER/EXPANDER
HOUSING

NAVIGATIONAL LIGHT

REAR THRUSTER
FOR 4-POD CONFIGURATION

RUNNING LIGHT

REACTION-CONTROL
THRUSTERS

NAVIGATIONAL SENSOR AND LIGHT

CARGO POD [2]

CARGO POD [2]

RUNNING LIGHTS

CARGO TRAIN ATTACHMENT

Enterprise's shuttlecraft hangar level, R Deck, is situated at the widest point of the secondary hull. Much of the deck consists of open space, as it is the midlevel of the cargo facility; thirty-two cargo pod modules may be stored in the alcoves lining the forward, port, and starboard sides of the bay.

At the forward end of the deck, behind the navigational deflector system, is the secondary auxiliary control center. This room, which encircles the vertical intermix chamber, enables command personnel to control all propulsive and shipboard systems should the primary hull suffer severe structural and control damage. Although destruction of this magnitude is unlikely, combat possibilities warrant such a backup facility.

Just aft of the control center is a compartment containing a reserve M-6B engineering control computer. This logic circuit, combined with the engineering computer on N Deck, provides sufficient regulation and memory to allow use of the ship's main warp drive system. The secondary auxiliary control center and the M-6B computer have their own emergency power supplies, which are located on the port and starboard sides of the forward secondary hull.

A secondary force field projection unit is mounted from deck-to-ceiling at a point between the cargo handling floor and the shuttlecraft elevators. This field retains the atmosphere in the cargo area at times when the landing bay is depressurized.

The shuttle hangar has sufficient room for the storage of four craft at any given time. During normal storage situations, these shuttlecraft face aftward.

Two cargo holds at the aft end of the level feature ceiling hatches which open into the landing bay floor.

R Deck also houses the vessel's lifeboat facilities. These one-man craft, which escape through blowaway panels in the side of the secondary hull, are provided for those persons who are unable to reach the primary hull before emergency separation takes place. Lifeboat operators in this event, once clear of the engineering section, are beamed aboard the saucer; if necessary, lifeboats may be taken aboard at the H Deck docking facility.

Lifeboat propulsion is provided by a series of particle-beam RCS units. Also, when it is necessary to get very far away from the secondary hull very quickly (as in the cases of self-destruct or engine overload), a forced ejection system in the side of the ship propels the lifeboat outward at a high rate of speed.

Cargo storage facility at R Deck level—note lifeboat station at right

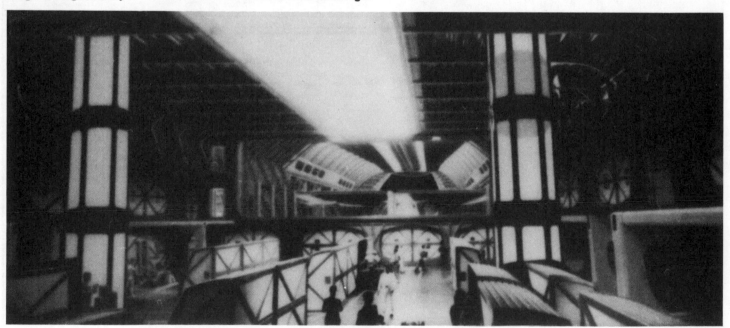

LIFEBOAT INSTRUCTIONS

1 Depress "open" switch on lifeboat exterior. Hatch will roll downward and lock into position.

2 Slide feet-first into lifeboat seat. Wait for green light to indicate that onboard computer has verified your presence. Say "personnel aboard" to close outer hatch. Blue light will indicate that hatch is locked and sealed.

3 Select "vocal" or "manual" control of lifeboat by depressing the appropriate switch on the operator's seat's right armrest.

4 If "vocal," say "Code One" to initiate ejection sequence. Five-second computer countdown will follow, after which forceful 4-G ejection will take place. Lifeboat will clear secondary hull's detonation radius after thirty seconds.

5 Say "Code Two" to initiate soft-departure sequence. Lifeboat will slide gently clear of the ship's hull, then to be controlled by the onboard RCS system. RCS maneuvers are controlled by using the joysticks on either side of the operator's seat.

6 Manual emergency ejection is initiated by pulling downward on the striped handle above the right armrest of the operator's seat.

7 Manual soft-departure is controlled using the joystick handles on each armrest.

8 Onboard air, food, and water supplies will last one person eight days. Power and propulsion systems will last for the same period of time with normal use.

9 A survival suit is stowed against the right-side bulkhead for use when the operator must leave the lifeboat while still within zero-atmosphere. Rotate turn-lock handle counter-clockwise to open coverplate of suit locker.

10 To leave lifeboat, say "Disembark" and pull inward on safety handle beside hatchway. Green light will come on and hatch will open.

LIFEBOAT (ELEVATION)

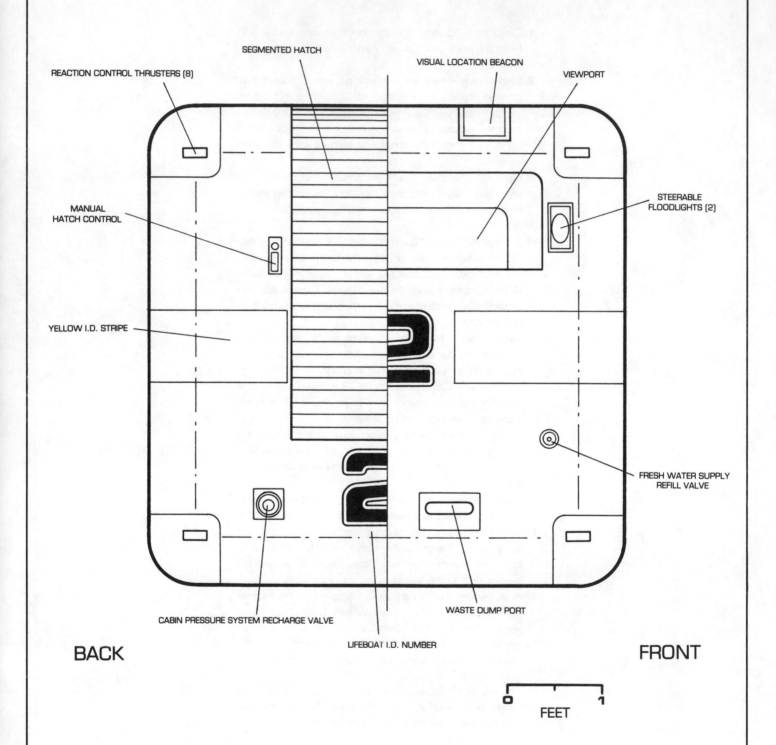

SEGMENTED HATCH

VISUAL LOCATION BEACON

VIEWPORT

REACTION CONTROL THRUSTERS (8)

STEERABLE
FLOODLIGHTS (2)

MANUAL
HATCH CONTROL

YELLOW I.D. STRIPE

FRESH WATER SUPPLY
REFILL VALVE

CABIN PRESSURE SYSTEM RECHARGE VALVE

WASTE DUMP PORT

LIFEBOAT I.D. NUMBER

BACK

FRONT

0   FEET   1

LIFEBOAT [SECTION]

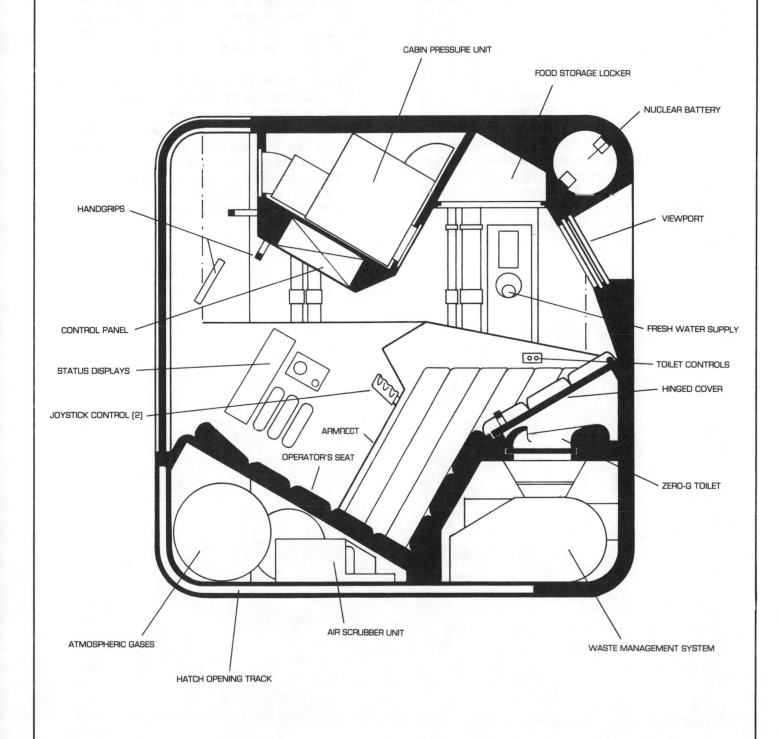

CABIN PRESSURE UNIT

FOOD STORAGE LOCKER

NUCLEAR BATTERY

HANDGRIPS

VIEWPORT

CONTROL PANEL

FRESH WATER SUPPLY

STATUS DISPLAYS

TOILET CONTROLS

HINGED COVER

JOYSTICK CONTROL [2]

ARMREST

OPERATOR'S SEAT

ZERO-G TOILET

ATMOSPHERIC GASES

AIR SCRUBBER UNIT

WASTE MANAGEMENT SYSTEM

HATCH OPENING TRACK

S Deck is often referred to simply as the "cargo deck." It is the main level of the cargo storage complex, and features alcove storage space for forty-eight cargo modules; additional modules can be stored by magnetic lock on the cargo loading floor itself. Just forward of the main storage area is a tandem cargo transporter facility, which is reached by passing through two sets of large double doors. Twin platforms are controlled from a common central room; loose cargo and large equipment are beamed aboard ship and carried by anti-grav to the appropriate shipboard destinations.

Three standard pads are provided on each platform for use by supervisory personnel who must oversee the transport of sensitive items. These pads are operated independently of the multisegmented cargo units.

The forward end of S Deck is occupied by a fabrication facility, similar to that on I Deck.

Aft of the cargo storage complex is the shuttlecraft maintenance shop. The two rectangular shuttle elevators normally resting at the R Deck level lower craft to be repaired to the shop floor. Parts storage lockers line the port and starboard bulkheads of the room, and contain replacement equipment for standard shuttlecraft, travel pods, and workbees.

S Deck is the lowest level that can be accessed by the main stairwell. Ladderways provide other means by which to reach T and U Decks.

Enterprise's recorder-marker launch system is mounted into the space between the shuttlecraft shop's rear bulkhead and the aft outer hull. These buoys are jettisoned prior to situations where the survival of the ship is uncertain, or when a ship under radio silence wishes to be tracked at a later date by Federation vessels.

CARGO TRANSPORTER COMPLEX

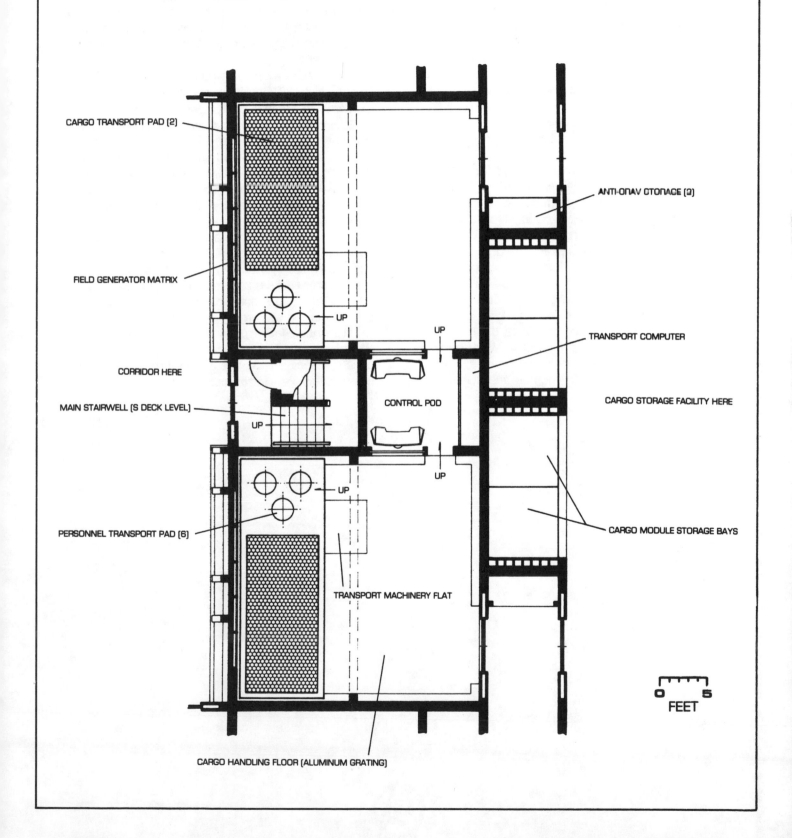

CARGO TRANSPORT PAD (2)

FIELD GENERATOR MATRIX

ANTI-GRAV STORAGE (2)

CORRIDOR HERE

TRANSPORT COMPUTER

MAIN STAIRWELL (S DECK LEVEL)

CARGO STORAGE FACILITY HERE

CONTROL POD

UP

PERSONNEL TRANSPORT PAD (6)

CARGO MODULE STORAGE BAYS

TRANSPORT MACHINERY FLAT

CARGO HANDLING FLOOR (ALUMINUM GRATING)

0   5
FEET

Occupying the forward end of T Deck, reaching from port to starboard, is Enterprise's matter/antimatter containment system. This specialized unit forms the base of the vertical intermix chamber and regulates the amount of fuel that flows into the shaft. Storage bottles affixed to the outside of the containment unit hold the matter and antimatter which powers the vessel; this fuel is kept in a plasma state and is insulated from the interior walls of the bottles by intense magnetic fields. Blow-away panels in the outer hull of the ship allow the antimatter storage bottles to be independently ejected into space should an emergency situation arise (such as magnetic field failure).

Just aft of the containment machinery, on the vessel centerline, is the tractor beam unit housing. Normally stowed retracted, the telescoping beam projector features a swivelling head which is shaped to form a flush seal with the outer hull.

Twelve panoramic viewports line the outer walls of the ship's botanical garden. This area, along with an adjoining botany laboratory, serves both the scientific and hobbyist requirements of shipboard personnel. A wide variety of plant life, in all shapes and colors, makes this area a favorite of off-duty personnel. Bench seating allows restful viewing of the garden and of space beyond the viewports, and a small snack bar is useful for games and conversation. A fresh-water stream and pond is stocked with many species of tropical fish, and features its own water supply and recirculating system.

A spacious messroom is connected to the garden by two corridors. This dining area has an adjoining specialty kitchen where crew members may prepare foods without the use of food processor machinery, if they wish.

Enterprise's swimming pool and sundeck fills out the aft third of T Deck. The regulation pool reaches a depth of twelve feet at one end, and gradually rises to three feet in the shallows. A diving board is available for personnel use.

Mounted onto the walls surrounding the pool and sundeck are a series of wraparound viewscreens. These may be programmed to display a variety of three-dimensional beach and island scenes which create a convincing illusion of Terran leave.

U Deck is the bottom level of the ship. A central corridor connects the sanitary wastes recovery room at the forward end of the deck with a series of fresh-water tanks and pump machinery rooms which line the port and starboard sides. At the aft end of the level is the swimming pool maintenance facility.

Enterprise's lower phaser banks are mounted into the superstructure beneath the U Deck floor. This phaser machinery may be reached through a pair of removable panels in the corridor flooring.

BOTANICAL GARDEN

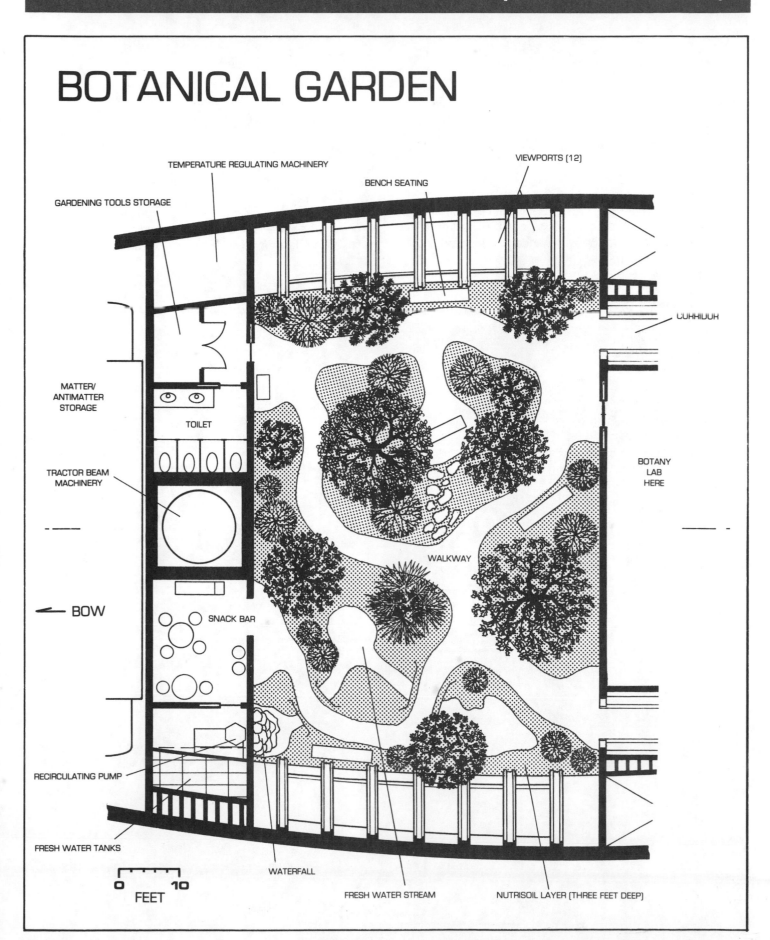

TEMPERATURE REGULATING MACHINERY

VIEWPORTS (12)

GARDENING TOOLS STORAGE

BENCH SEATING

CORRIDOR

MATTER/
ANTIMATTER
STORAGE

TOILET

BOTANY
LAB
HERE

TRACTOR BEAM
MACHINERY

WALKWAY

← BOW

SNACK BAR

RECIRCULATING PUMP

0   10
FEET

FRESH WATER TANKS

WATERFALL

FRESH WATER STREAM

NUTRISOIL LAYER (THREE FEET DEEP)

APPENDIX

ENTERPRISE NCC-1701-A

Star Fleet's Enterprise Class vessels are the most powerful in space today. Since their initial launching in 2217, they have proven to be the United Federation of Planets' most effective deterrent to hostile attack. Extensive research capabilities and unmatched combat readiness make them the most versatile of all vessels currently in service, and as such the Enterprise Class has become the primary strength of the Federation, much as the Constitution Class once was.

For this reason, most new developments in spaceflight and weapons technology are first tested for their compatibility with Enterprise Class ships. Cruisers of this class are produced at the orbital Terran and Salazaar shipyards at a rate of four per year, allowing much flexibility in the testing of improved and new systems.

The most dramatic and promising development in many years is the discovery of what has come to be known as transwarp drive. This new propulsion technology is based upon a discovery made several years earlier by the U.S.S. Enterprise while in an area which borders on Tholian space.

Enterprise's sensors recorded a natural phenomena never before known; Science Officer Spock carefully documented a "doorway" between two parallel planes of existence, which he labelled an "interphase." This "tear" in the fabric of three-dimensional space-time was found to create, following prolonged exposure, an imbalance in the chemical composition of neural and muscular tissues in human beings, causing insanity and ultimately death; this effect killed the crew of the starship Defiant, which drifted through the interphase ahead of Enterprise.

This natural "tear" proved to Federation scientists that travel between dimensional planes was possible, and research began into the possibility of generating an artificial interphase for travel purposes. Enterprise's sensors had recorded that time flowed at a different rate in parallel space, and that that plane of existence was devoid of all matter and energy, providing an obstacle-free course of travel.

Theoretically, a starship could drop into parallel space and move on a preset course for a predetermined period of time, then drop back into normal space once the destination coordinates had been reached. Because of the time differential, shipboard travel time would vary greatly from the passage of time in normal space; a vessel might undertake a three-week voyage to a distant star system, only to find after arrival that four days had passed in normal space. While the ship actually moved no faster than was possible with standard warp drive, the relative effect would be that of making a three-week trip in four days, giving the same end result as would be provided by vastly increased warp speeds. Such warp speeds would create stresses beyond the tolerances of any conceivable structural design or building material, destroying any ship which attempted them.

So, it was concluded, a "shortcut" existed which could open up entirely new areas of space for exploration. After nearly twelve years of intensive research and development, two drive system producers felt that they had each designed the most feasible warp field configuration for interphase travel. Both designs combined intricate warp and transporter field matrices to generate a momentary "doorway" through which the equipped vessel could enter parallel space. This artificial interphase would be of such short duration that even repeated exposure would be harmless to the ship's crew, avoiding the effects suffered by Defiant.

The first "transwarp" engines actually constructed were built by Shuvinaaljis Warp Technologies. Only two were constructed, and both were mounted onto Star Fleet's newest battleship, Excelsior, for field testing. These nacelles are huge, with each having twice the mass and being double the length of Enterprise's FWG-1 units. At this time, these engines are still being simulator-tested within the Terran orbital space dock facility.

The other entry into the transwarp race was developed at Leeding Engines, Ltd., and consisted of similar field generation machinery, on a smaller scale, which was mounted into an FWG-1 housing. The Leeding nacelles were finally constructed several months after those from Shuvinaaljis were ready to be ship-mounted, and as a result Leeding lost out as supplier for the Excelsior class. However, Star Fleet's Board of Engineers liked the smaller and more customary design, and it was decided that the new FTWG-1 would be tested on an Enterprise class starship.

The U.S.S. Ti-Ho was chosen to be the host vessel for the new drive design. Ti-Ho was not a Constitution refit, but was built new from the keel up. The new M-6 Mark II computer, used successfully on starships Saratoga II and Kitty Hawk, performed perfectly as the logic system for Leeding's transwarp design and was installed on Ti-Ho.

Six months prior to her scheduled completion, Ti-

MAIN BRIDGE

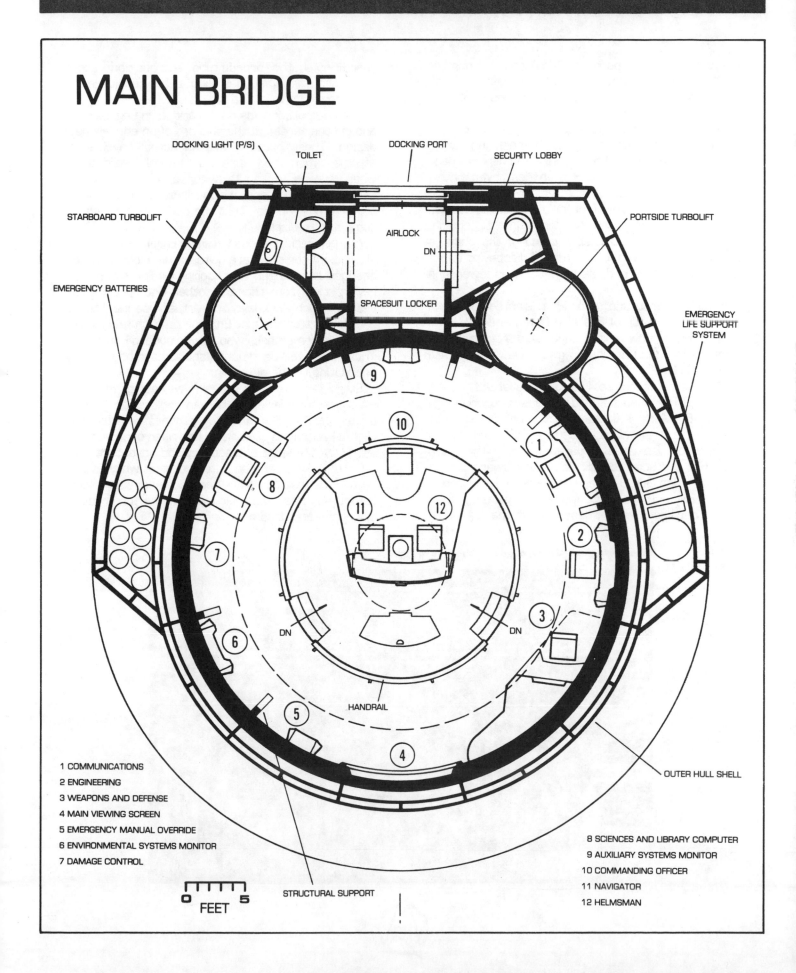

DOCKING LIGHT (P/S)

TOILET

DOCKING PORT

SECURITY LOBBY

STARBOARD TURBOLIFT

AIRLOCK

DN

PORTSIDE TURBOLIFT

EMERGENCY BATTERIES

SPACESUIT LOCKER

EMERGENCY LIFE SUPPORT SYSTEM

DN

DN

HANDRAIL

OUTER HULL SHELL

1 COMMUNICATIONS
2 ENGINEERING
3 WEAPONS AND DEFENSE
4 MAIN VIEWING SCREEN
5 EMERGENCY MANUAL OVERRIDE
6 ENVIRONMENTAL SYSTEMS MONITOR
7 DAMAGE CONTROL

8 SCIENCES AND LIBRARY COMPUTER
9 AUXILIARY SYSTEMS MONITOR
10 COMMANDING OFFICER
11 NAVIGATOR
12 HELMSMAN

STRUCTURAL SUPPORT

0 FEET 5

Ho was issued her permanent hull registry number (NCC-1798) and final computer simulations took place which verified the effectiveness of her transwarp drive.

Then, on September 21, 2222, as Ti-Ho returned from her deep-space trials, the "Whalesong" crisis took place. Admiral James T. Kirk and his command crew, who had stolen and then destroyed Enterprise, returned to Earth from Vulcan and, using the time-speed breakaway factor, managed to resolve the crisis and safeguard the planet. In appreciation, the Federation dropped all but one of the charges against Kirk; he was found guilty of disobeying direct Star Fleet orders and, as a result, was lowered in rank to Captain.

In further gratitude, Star Fleet elected to return Kirk to the position of Starship Commander, and he was given a new ship; Ti-Ho was re-christened "Enterprise" and her hull registry was changed to NCC-1701-A.

This new Enterprise is truly a state-of-the-art vessel. Other than Leeding's transwarp drive and her M-6 Mark II logic center, Enterprise also features a transwarp subspace communications system for use while in parallel space. This radio capability is crucial, for at relative transwarp speeds (greater than 3000 times the speed of light) Enterprise easily outruns conventional subspace signals.

Another improvement designed into the vessel is a rear-firing photon torpedo tube. This additional stern firing arc fills what has long been considered a dangerous gunnery blind spot.

The control consoles on the bridge, in engineering, and in other areas of the ship are of an entirely new design. These boards have no actual physical instrumentation, and appear a smooth, solid black when turned off; all switches are computer-generated touch pads, which allows each console to perform any function that the user asks the ship's computer to display.

Any other differences between Enterprise and her previous sister ships are quite minor. Only cosmetic changes in bulkhead and flooring design distinguish her interior from those of other Enterprise class vessels; each deck layout is virtually identical to its counterpart on the last Enterprise, with few exceptions. Crew members who served aboard Enterprise prior to her self-destruction should have no difficulty in adapting to the new ship.

Star Fleet's newest vessel is well-equipped to expand the boundaries of human exploration. Enterprise, the flagship and key ambassador for the United Federation of Planets, has risen once again to symbolize the spirit of discovery and adventure that has always driven humanity to seek that which is just beyond its reach. With her renewed youth, this gallant lady has taken her place at the forefront of our hopes and dreams.

Enterprise department heads on the new bridge

The redesigned communications station

The auxiliary systems monitoring station

DEDICATION PLAQUE
[MOUNTED IN MAIN BRIDGE STBD TURBOLIFT ALCOVE]

USS ENTERPRISE

STARSHIP CLASS
SAN FRANCISCO, CALIF.
UNITED FEDERATION
OF PLANETS

". . . to boldly go
where no man has gone before."

– from the Starfleet charter

Enterprise preparing to get underway (December 21, 2222)

BRIDGE DISPLAY GRAPHICS

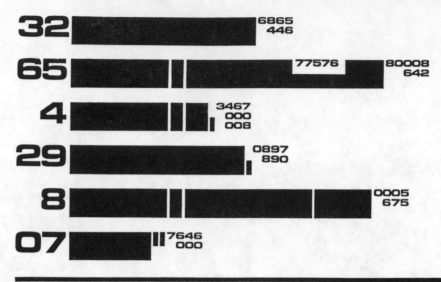

32 6865 446

65 77576 80008 642

4 3467 000 008

29 0897 890

8 0005 675

07 7646 000

LIFE SUPPORT RESERVES 513   **8 9605**

LIFE SUPPORT RESERVES
Monitors status and availability of key life-support consumables as compared to current demand. On operator command, can overlay projected consumption rates and display mean-time to exhaustion.

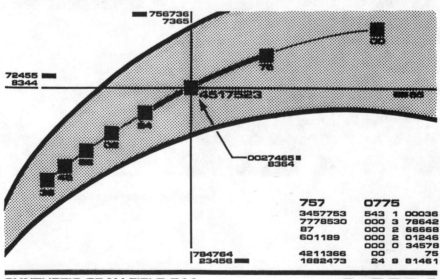

SYNTHETIC GRAV FIELD 514   **6 2894**

SYNTHETIC GRAV FIELD
Monitors field values of ship's artificial gravity system and shows interaction with inertial damping field. Alerts operator when inertial potential difference exceeds 127 m/s² over current velocity.

ENVIRONMENTAL SYSTEMS MONITOR

INFORMATION SUBSYSTEMS MONITOR 3-1797

Displays relative priorities of high-density information processing flow. Indicates availability of various processing subsystems.

3 1797
PRIORITY 503

```
86  43  10198
53  89  75421
13  88    188
21  00  00000
 4  21   4567
30   8  75310
40  02  16786
```

0 4436
ONLINE 505

```
86  6  5210240002
52  6  3140246
 6  4  000246310

75  2
00  4

31  0
43  1
 9  7
```

SENSOR ARRAY MONITOR 0-4436

Displays status of certain sensor array subsystems tied through the library computer network. Shows current sensor information processing configuration.

SCIENCES

BRIDGE DISPLAY GRAPHICS

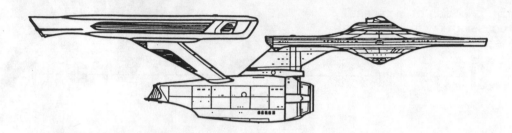

3578			6500	765543		
543	100	036	753223457753	543	1	00036
000	357	642	002467778530	000	3	78642
000	246	668	6549987	000	2	66668
000	200	246	31202601189	000	2	01246
				000	0	34578
000	586	075	898754211366	00		75
24	998	461	886421882473	24	9	81461
001	577	642	0000000035	01	5	76642
024	78	765	212345678	24	6	88765
553	36	643	589753100023	53	0	7643
864	2	024	024167864149	64	8	1024
524	1	024	86000	24	4	14024

STRUCTURAL INTEGRITY 515   **5 2536**

STRUCTURAL INTEGRITY

Displays mechanical stress values for key structural points. On operator command, can overlay inertial field structural reinforcement and/or projected failure points and times.

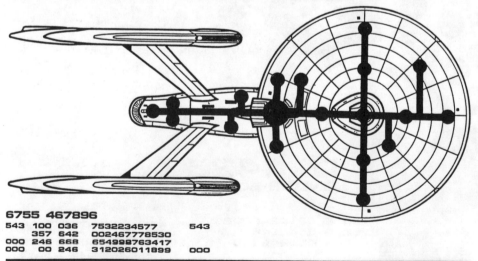

6755	467896			
543	100	036	7532234577	543
	357	642	002467778530	
000	246	668	654999763417	
000	00	246	312026011899	000

AUX POWER DISTRIB 516   **5 3312**

AUX POWER DISTRIB

Displays allocation and distribution of emergency power system. Also shows relative consumption rates of priority systems.

DAMAGE CONTROL

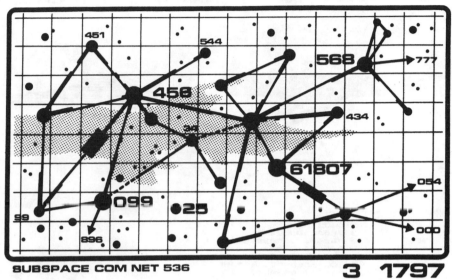

SUBSPACE COM NET 536   3 1797

SUBSPACE COM NET
Displays local traffic pattern of subspace communications network. Indicates relative traffic loads for various comm nodes and transmission availability.

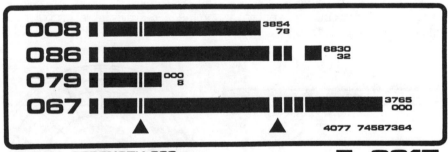

SIGNAL STRENGTH 000   5 0217

SIGNAL STRENGTH
Shows signal/noise ratio of primary subspace comm channels currently in use for net interface or ship-ship communications. Alerts operator when signal quality falls below values required for current transmission mode.

34 00075					64 545157890					
543	10	00	68	75	024	6 8	76	43	0000	0345786543210198 4323
000	35	86	21	00	53	0 6	4	01	0003	86007536898
0	4	66		5	864	2	2	00	46	98146137886421882
000	20	12		31	524	4	02	67	013	776642100000000

HAILING FREQUENCIES 537   5 1702

HAILING FREQUENCIES
Displays current frequency assignments and hailing protocols.

COMMUNICATIONS

BRIDGE DISPLAY GRAPHICS

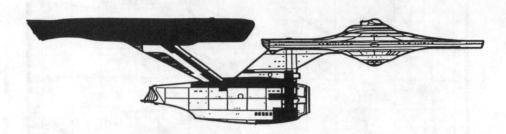

```
758        8900007
36  410    543 1  0003689753223457753
54  210    000 3  78642100024677
00   35    000 2  6666887654998763
00  024    000    012465431202
00  020     00 0  345786543210198432
00  000        5  6007536898754211366
 0  358    424 9  8146137884218
 2   99    001 5  766421000000
00  357     24 6  8876543212334567865
02    7    553    67643015897531
 5  103    864 8  2102400024167864149
86  685      4 4  1402467860000002402
```

TRANSWARP SUBSYS 525   **7 4516**

TRANSWARP SUBSYS
Displays status of primary transwarp subsystems. Indicates flux values of
antimatter intermix core. On operator command, can overlay intercooler rates
and field generator output.

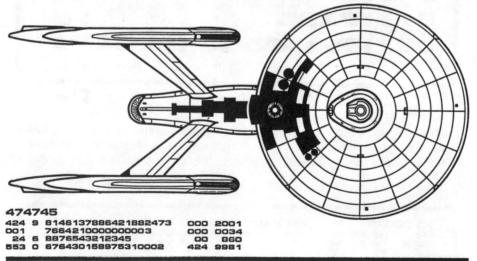

```
474745
424 9  8146137886421882473    000  2001
001    7664210000000003        000  0034
 24 6  8876543212345            00   860
553 0  67643015897531000002    424  9981
```

IMPULSE SUBSYS 526   **3 4166**

IMPULSE SUBSYS
Displays status of primary impulse drive subsystems. Shows fusion reactor
status and deuterium consumption rates.

ENGINEERING

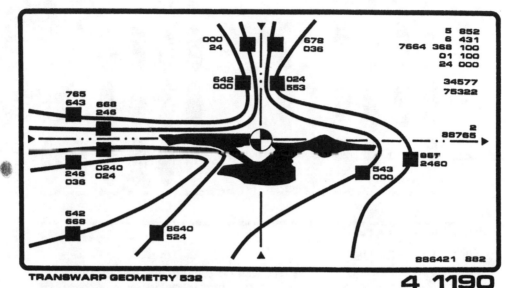

TRANSWARP GEOMETRY 532

4 1190

TRANSWARP GEOMETRY

Displays warp field configuration and subspace flow rates at selected points.
On operator command, can overlay nominal warp geometry and display field
differences.

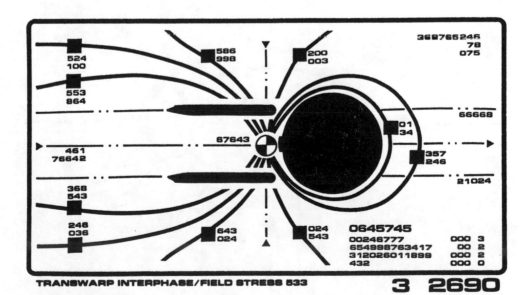

TRANSWARP INTERPHASE/FIELD STRESS 533

3 2690

FIELD STRESS

Shows warp field stress with relationship to ideal subspace flow. Also shows
flow rates at selected points with respect to direction of travel.

ENGINEERING

BRIDGE DISPLAY GRAPHICS

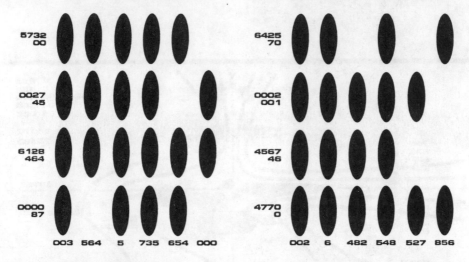

DILITHIUM STATUS 531   7 8648

DILITHIUM STATUS

Monitors condition of primary dilithium core elements and shows projected decrystallization rates. Alerts operator when decay rates exceed 107% of nominal.

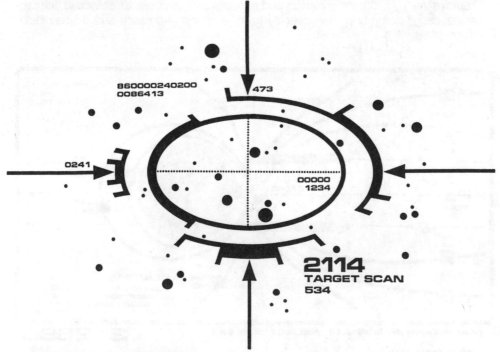

WEAPONS AND DEFENSE

Tactical display of targeted object(s), corrected for relativistic or warp field disortion. Indicates available field correction factors for phaser targeting, and shows probable evasion patterns.

WEAPONS AND DEFENSE

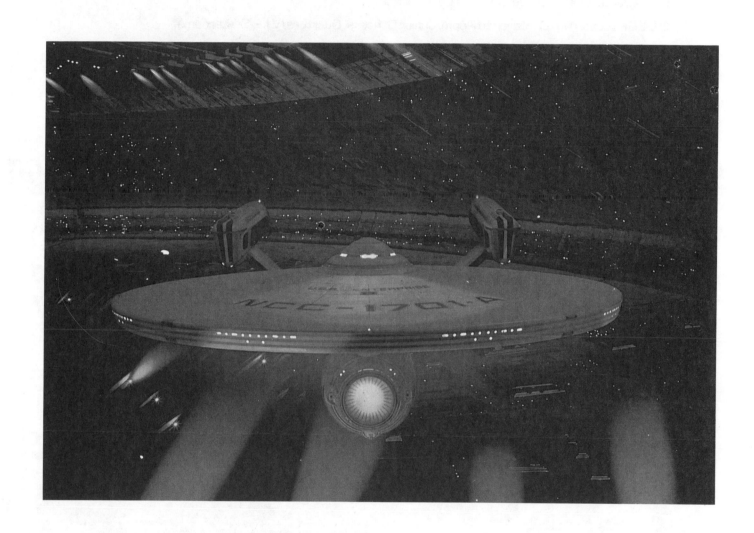

SHIP'S DIRECTORY

A DECK [BRIDGE] (Level 1)—Main bridge/V.I.P. Docking Port

B DECK (Level 2)—Main Security Level/Security Chief's Office

C DECK (Level 3)—Officers' (V.I.P.) Lounge/Mess

D DECK (Level 4)—Conference Room/Junior Officers' Quarters/V.I.P. Staterooms

E DECK (Level 5)—Senior Officers' Quarters

F DECK (Level 6)—Crew's Quarters/Crew's Messrooms/Crew's Lounge/Elevator Maintenance Shop/Impulse Engineering

G [MAIN] DECK (Level 7)—Armory/Auxiliary Control/Chapel/Gymnasium/Main Briefing Room/Main Brig/Rec Deck/Science Labs/Sickbay/Transporter Complex

H-I DECKS (Levels 8-9)—Auxiliary Fire Control/Departure Lounge/Docking Port Complex/Fabrication Center

J DECK (Level 10)—Primary Hull Circuit Breaker Room

K DECK (Level 11)—Main Sensor Array Monitoring Station

L-M DECKS (Levels 12-13)—Photon Torpedo Launching System

N-O [ENGINEERING] DECKS (Levels 14-15)—Warp Engineering

P-Q DECKS (Levels 16-17)—Emergency Transporters/Engineering Support/Engineering Offices/Landing Bay/Maintenance

R DECK (Level 18)—Shuttlecraft Hangar

S DECK (Level 19)—Cargo Deck/Cargo Transporter Complex

T-U DECKS (Levels 20-21)—Botanical Garden/Crew's Messroom /Matter-Antimatter Containment Facility / Pool

INDEX